**Ian's eyes flew ope[n]
Shannon, yanking her to the floor,
crushing her beneath him as he swept
his pistol back and forth toward the
room around them.**

"What is it?" he demanded. "What happened?"

"Ian, it's just me." Shannon's voice came out a harsh croak. She cleared her throat. "There's no one else here."

He frowned and looked down at her. "You're okay?"

She pressed shaking hands against his chest, an unexpected rush of tears clogging her throat. How could she have ever doubted this man? He was shielding her with his body, thinking someone was there to hurt her. He was willing to give his life for hers. The enormity of that knowledge had the tears flowing down her cheeks.

He shoved his pistol back into the holster and pulled her up with him, his concerned gaze searching hers. "I'm so sorry. I didn't mean to frighten you."

"Frighten me?" She laughed and wiped away her tears. "You scared me nearly to death. But that's not why I'm crying. You shielded me with your body, trying to protect me, even after how badly I treated you."

UNDERCOVER REBEL

Lena Diaz

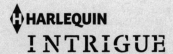

Thank you to all the wonderful readers enjoying this series, especially those who have sent me emails and messages about how much they love this special family of law-enforcement heroes. I hope Ian's story warms your heart and leaves you with a smile on your face.

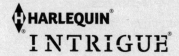

ISBN-13: 978-1-335-13563-6

Recycling programs for this product may not exist in your area.

Undercover Rebel

Copyright © 2020 by Lena Diaz

This edition published by arrangement with Harlequin Books S.A.

For questions and comments about the quality of this book, please contact us at CustomerService@Harlequin.com.

Harlequin Enterprises ULC
22 Adelaide St. West, 40th Floor
Toronto, Ontario M5H 4E3, Canada
www.Harlequin.com

Printed in U.S.A.

Lena Diaz was born in Kentucky and has also lived in California, Louisiana and Florida, where she now resides with her husband and two children. Before becoming a romantic suspense author, she was a computer programmer. A Romance Writers of America Golden Heart® Award finalist, she has also won the prestigious Daphne du Maurier Award for Excellence in Mystery/Suspense. To get the latest news about Lena, please visit her website, lenadiaz.com.

Books by Lena Diaz

Harlequin Intrigue

The Mighty McKenzies

Smoky Mountains Ranger
Smokies Special Agent
Conflicting Evidence
Undercover Rebel

Tennessee SWAT

Mountain Witness
Secret Stalker
Stranded with the Detective
SWAT Standoff

Marshland Justice

Missing in the Glades
Arresting Developments
Deep Cover Detective
Hostage Negotiation

The Marshal's Witness
Explosive Attraction
Undercover Twin
Tennessee Takedown
The Bodyguard

Visit the Author Profile page at Harlequin.com.

CAST OF CHARACTERS

Ian McKenzie—The rebellious youngest McKenzie, Ian is driven to atone for the mistakes of his past by risking his life deep undercover saving victims of human trafficking.

Shannon Murphy—She escaped a life on the streets and is desperate to save the friend that she had to leave behind. Can she overcome her justified fears of law enforcement when she discovers Ian's true identity? Or will her fears be the death of both of them?

Cameron Ellison—Is it true this assistant district attorney has ties to the main suspect in the human trafficking ring?

Barry Nash—Someone seems to be spilling information to the traffickers that Ian is trying to catch. Could it be his boss at Homeland Security?

Chris Parker—Ian's undercover liaison. Could he be the reason the traffickers seem to know Ian's next steps before he takes them?

Wolverine—Wolverine is Ian's intermediary to make deals with the head of the human trafficking ring. But Wolverine's interest in Shannon just might get her killed.

Butch—Everything hinges on whether this man can be tricked into trusting the undercover agent. But if he even suspects Ian's true identity, everything will be lost.

Chapter One

Ian spotted his target in the back-left corner of the truck stop's massive parking lot, parked sideways as if poised for a quick getaway. Two empty spaces separated the white panel van from a garish bright yellow semi, one of dozens of rigs parked along the chain-link fence. He couldn't help rolling his eyes at the cliché of bad guys in a panel van. Just once he'd like to come up against his prey driving something more original with a cool factor, like a sports car, or even a blacked-out Suburban if they had to go big. Then again, a fancy car would attract attention, and attention was the last thing they wanted. It was the last thing *Ian* wanted.

He hunched his leather jacket against the cold wind blowing down from the Tennessee side of the Smoky Mountains and started forward. A glance to his right revealed the fast-food drive-through was already beginning to bustle with people looking for a quick, easy supper. Harassed-looking moms and dads in SUVs placed their orders, kids in the back yelling, laughing or crying through the open windows. None of them seemed to notice what was *really* going on outside the reach of the restaurant's neon glow. Few people ever did.

Rigs belched smoke behind the restaurant, pulling up to lines of diesel fuel pumps that seemed to go on forever. Others parked to catch a few hours of sleep before getting back on I-40 to head into nearby Gatlinburg or some other destination. The occasional achingly young woman or man hopped in and out of the various sleeper cabs, sometimes pausing to grab junk food right alongside the soccer moms and dads inside the restaurant. And no one thought twice about it. Which was why business thrived out here. Just not the kind of business most of the decent people in this part of Tennessee knew about. Or the average person in hundreds of other towns just like this one.

Sometimes Ian wondered why he bothered to fight anymore. The odds were overwhelmingly against him. More often than not, his missions ended in defeat rather than victory. But every time he was on the verge of quitting, the memories would slam into him. Dormant grief and anger would work their way through his system like banked coals igniting into a dangerous wildfire. And then a name would prick his conscience.

Willow.

That was his battle cry, a reminder of his greatest failure, the reason he persevered even when the odds of making a difference seemed pathetically out of reach. But it was a newer name that pushed him forward tonight—*Maria.* Although he didn't know her, his friend and neighbor Shannon did. And the word on the street was that the men he was about to meet knew Maria too.

But they weren't her friends.

Ian sent up a silent prayer that Shannon would be uncharacteristically patient, that she'd stay in his car as she'd promised when this opportunity came up. They'd been on their way to a pizza joint when the long-awaited call had come in. If he'd taken the time to drive her home, he'd have missed the meeting. And neither of them had been willing to risk that.

Up ahead, a twentysomething skinny white guy with dark greasy hair and ragged jeans waved at Ian from near the van's front bumper. The kid had dubbed himself Wolverine. But something more passive, like Archie or Howard, seemed more appropriate. He didn't exactly inspire fear. But he did have his uses—like setting up tonight's meeting.

"Hurry up, Ian." Wolverine wrung his hands and glanced at the trio standing beside the van's closed sliding door. "The boss doesn't have all day."

Ian kept his steady, unhurried pace. It gave him time to size up his adversaries. According to Wolverine, their names were Butch, Jagger and Axel. Ian would bet the .357 Magnum Ruger GP100 that he'd left in his car for Shannon's protection that those monikers were just as fake as Wolverine's. But unlike Wolverine, these men's nicknames fit them perfectly. And they didn't give the impression that they were the least bit worried about Ian's size.

At six-one, his height tended to be an advantage when facing an opponent. But it was his powerful biceps and muscular physique that usually gave him the intimidation edge. His leather jacket, spiky black-and-blond hair, and dragon tattoos peeking out from his neck and wrists completed his street image. But the bulked-up men calmly watching him approach had Ian thinking he should up his reps at the gym. A lot. If things went south in the next few minutes, he might end up in the fight of his life. And that was only if they didn't kill each other in a shoot-out first.

"Lose the shades." The biggest of the three gave the order. His red hair and pale, freckled skin probably got him teased when he was younger. No one would make that mistake now. He could have been the Incredible Hulk's younger, less green brother, with a carrot top.

"And take your hands out of your pockets." That from the middle guy. Ian half expected the dark-skinned giant to pull a sword from behind his back and go all daywalker on him like Wesley Snipes in the *Blade* movies.

Ian kept his hands in his pockets. He didn't take off his shades. He looked to number three and jerked his head toward his fellow thugs. "I get the Incredible Hulk and Blade. But who are you supposed to be? Captain Jack Sparrow, on steroids?"

Jack's eyes widened, and he looked to his boss as if to take his lead on a response. Ian chalked him up as a minion, like Wolverine. No one important. He focused his attention on the other two. It was Blade who straightened, tossing his dreads and baring his white teeth like a hungry pit bull. First lieutenant, then, the main man's bodyguard. Definitely important. And dangerous.

"You think you're funny or something?" Blade flexed his fists at his sides.

"What are you doing, Ian?" Wolverine sounded like he was ready to faint. "You tryin' to get yourself killed?"

Zeroing in on the one he'd come for, Ian stopped three feet away from Hulk. He kept his left hand in his jacket pocket wrapped around the butt of his second-favorite gun, a Glock .22. Not as powerful or impressive-looking as his .357 revolver, it had the advantage of holding more rounds with less recoil. And it fit perfectly in his pocket. He could take out Blade and Jack without even pulling out the gun. But it would ruin a really nice jacket.

He stared directly at Hulk. "This macho drama is great if you're trying to intimidate some green kid straight out of high school. But I'm not green, and high school was a long time ago. My buyers are impatient for some fresh product. I was told you were the guy who could get it. Either show me what you have or my money and I go elsewhere."

"Ian, man. You're blowin' it." Wolverine sidled closer to Hulk. "You need to show some respect and—"

Hulk held up his hand. Wolverine slunk to the front of the van again. Blade had moved forward when Ian had. But he stepped back at his boss's signal, looking none too happy about it. Jack's eyes seemed to bulge from their sockets as he glared at Ian. Apparently, he wasn't a fan of Captain Jack Sparrow. That alone had Ian wanting to knock some sense into him.

"How fresh are we talking?" Hulk's voice was deathly quiet, his dark gaze riveted on Ian.

"I don't make deals with people I don't know." Ian slowly and deliberately pulled his right hand out of his pocket, then held it out toward the leader. "Ian Savage."

Hulk eyed his hand for a long moment. Time seemed to stand still as Ian waited. In his peripheral vision, he watched for sudden movements from the others, calculating distances and reaction times as he sifted through various possible scenarios.

"The name's Butch." Hulk finally grasped Ian's hand in a firm handshake. When he let go, he waved toward his lieutenant. "That's Axel, and over there is Jagger." The corner of his mouth lifted. "But I kind of like Blade and Sparrow. Might have to borrow those." He chuckled and reached into his pocket.

Ian tensed. Butch noticed and hesitated. He mimicked Ian's earlier slow, deliberate movements as he pulled his hand out of his pocket, revealing a stack of photographs.

"Product." Butch's mouth curved into a lecherous grin. "The freshest around. Your buyers have any particular preferences, fetishes?" He fanned out the pictures like he was playing poker, and held them up in the air. "Redheads, blondes, brunettes. Tall, short, skinny, fat. I've got 'em all."

Ian flicked his gaze over each of the pictures. None of them matched Maria's description or had the tattoo on her neck that Shannon had told him about. "Got any Latinas? Dark hair, dark eyes? Curvy?"

Butch shrugged, his smile fading. "I got a few. But they're older, more...experienced. I thought your buyer wanted fresh."

Ian made a quick course correction, forcing a grin as he worked to keep his worm on the hook. "The Latina would be a bonus, for me."

Butch laughed, biting at the bait again. "If we deal, maybe I'll throw *two* Spanish beauties in just for you. What about your buyer? What's his preference?"

"Young," Ian said. "*Very* young."

"A man after my own tastes." He winked.

The urge to slam the butt of his pistol against the pervert's grinning mouth was nearly overwhelming. Instead, Ian schooled his features into a bland expression that gave nothing away of the turmoil inside him.

Butch pulled a smaller stack of pictures from his other pocket and made a show of licking his lips before turning them face out. "Young enough for you?" His brow arched. "I mean, for your friend, of course."

Bile rose in Ian's throat. The girls in the photographs didn't look old enough to be in high school. Two were prepubescent. He tightened his grip on the pistol in his pocket. One little squeeze and he could rid the world of this piece of garbage. But that wouldn't help the victims in those photographs. Until he knew where they were, he had to treat this animal like a human being.

Forcing a conspiratorial grin was beyond Ian's abilities. "How fast can you deliver?"

"A couple of hours. If the price is right."

Disappointment shot through him. He'd hoped the victims were close by, maybe hidden in the back of one of the big rigs. The whole mission could have been resolved in minutes. The young girls—none of them were old enough to be called women— could be rescued from this scum's depraved clutches and given a new chance at the life they deserved. Instead, he'd have to keep up the facade a little longer.

He held out his hand to take possession of the photographs. "I need a closer look before I choose."

"They're all A1 prime. I take good care of my girls." Another lascivious grin. "You pick the ones you're interested in. Then we talk price and delivery." Butch stacked the pictures together and held them out.

"Ian? Ian, is that you?" a man called out from behind him.

Ian froze. *No.* Of all people to recognize him from his other life, why did it have to be *him*? He was going to ruin everything.

He reached for the pictures.

Butch snatched them back, and suddenly Ian was looking down the bore of a pistol.

Chapter Two

Ian bit back a curse. "What are you doing, Butch? You threaten all your potential buyers?"

He'd been close, so close. He *needed* those pictures. He *needed* the trust of this monster pointing the pistol at him. And now a chance encounter with someone from his *other* life was jeopardizing months of undercover work, and the anticipated rescue of Hulk's young victims.

"You a cop, Ian?" Butch's knuckles whitened on the pistol grip. "'Cause that guy calling your name smells like a cop to me. You trying to pull something?"

Ian leaned slightly forward, curling his lip in derision even as he felt a bead of sweat roll down the back of his neck. "Don't insult me by calling me names. I ain't no cop."

Hulk studied him as if trying to decide whether to believe him. He subtly jerked his head. Axel and Blade slid the side door open behind him and hopped inside the van. Wolverine jumped into the passenger seat up front.

"Ian!" the voice called out again, closer.

Think fast. You can fix this. You have *to fix this.*

Butch looked past Ian's shoulder, then pocketed his gun. "That guy looks familiar. Who is he?"

Ian was seriously sweating now. Did Butch have a run-in with Adam in the past? Would he remember where he saw him? He went all in, and prayed his bluff would work. He jerked his thumb over his shoulder.

"That's the piece of crap who screwed my girlfriend. I'll get rid of him. Then you and I can finish business."

He whirled and strode toward Adam, half expecting to feel the burn of a bullet between his shoulders. He funneled all of his frustration and anger into an expression of pure malice as he glared at the man who was endangering everything. Of all the people to recognize him and interrupt his mission, why did it have to be Adam? He was two inches taller than Ian, if not more muscular. And, naturally, he was standing beside a cool blacked-out SUV that he must have parked when he saw Ian.

He didn't stop until he was right in Adam's face. "Punch me." His voice was pitched low so no one else would hear. "Hard."

"Punch you? Why would I punch—"

Ian slugged him in the jaw, spinning him around. He followed up with a solid left hook to the middle, making him double over.

Adam coughed, his eyes watering as he glared up at Ian. He slowly straightened and wiped a thin trickle of blood from the corner of his mouth. "You want to give me one good reason why I shouldn't beat the crap out of you for that?"

"Nope." Ian braced himself for what he knew was coming, and slowly drew back his fist again, giving Adam plenty of opportunity. The punch caught him in the shoulder like a battering ram, slamming him to the pavement. His head bounced against the concrete and his mouth filled with blood. Holy hell. He'd forgotten just how strong Adam was. The man was built like a bull.

Somewhere behind him laughter sounded. Some truckers watching the fun? Or Butch and his crew? An engine revved. The van. Ian's stomach sank. He'd lost his opportunity to rescue the girls, at least tonight. He shook his head, desperately trying to clear his double vision as he pushed himself to his feet. Maybe Butch would give him another chance. Ian had to convince him this fight was for real, and that Adam wasn't a cop. He had to keep this up until the van was gone. Even if it killed him.

He spit out a stream of blood and turned, then ducked just in time to avoid a fist to the face.

The white van pulled out of its spot, slowly passing them. Butch was definitely watching. Ian had to make this convincing.

He straightened, both fists in front of him as he tried to figure out which blurry image to hit. He made a half-hearted jab toward the middle one, then braced himself for the return punch. It was a one-two combo, making him double over from the first hit, then spin around with the second. He wobbled, the white of the van barely in his field of vision now. They were still watching. Was that a good thing? Or a bad thing? Were bullets about to fly or was Butch going to lie low and set up a new meeting later?

One more weak jab at Adam hit air as planned. Even knowing what was coming, he wasn't prepared for the violence of the return punch. It slammed into his ribs, knocking the wind out of him and sending him flying backward.

He managed to cover his head with his arm this time before he hit the concrete.

Fiery lava shot up his left arm and zinged through his shoulder. The only thing that kept him from shouting was a mouthful of blood. He spit again, then coughed and rolled onto his stomach, trying to push himself up on all fours. His left arm hung useless at his side. He swore. How was he supposed to go up against thugs like the Hulk with a bum shooting arm? Maybe he should have slugged Adam for real. He might have lost more by throwing this fight than he'd gained.

"Ian, good grief. Stay down. I'll call an ambulance."

"No." He coughed up more blood. "No ambulance." At least, that was what he tried to say. He was pretty sure it came out something like "nolnce."

The van sped off.

Thank God.

Adam crouched in front of him, a little unsteady himself, seeming to favor his left leg even though Ian didn't think he'd hit it. "Be still. Quit trying to stand." He pulled out his phone. "I'll call—"

Tires screeched. An engine roared.

"What the—" Adam jumped back to avoid being hit by Ian's black Dodge Charger.

Ah, hell.

"Hey, big bully. Back off. Now," Shannon called through the open window. "Ian, get in." The passenger door popped open beside him. "Stay back, jerk, or I'll put a hole in you."

Ian squinted toward the car. She was pointing his .357 Magnum at Adam. Things had just gone from bad to about ten levels worse than that. He wobbled to his feet just as Adam brought up his Glock.

"Drop it, lady," Adam ordered.

Ian staggered between them, using his body as a shield, hoping they both didn't start a shoot-out with him in the middle. He rarely wore a Kevlar vest while undercover, just in case a bad guy wanted to see proof that he wasn't wearing a wire. Now he was reconsidering the sanity of that decision.

"Ergmrph." He shook his head in defeat. Either his brain was scrambled or the cut in his mouth was garbling his words. Probably both.

"Ian, get out of the way." Adam jerked his gun down.

Progress.

He forced his uncooperative legs to shuffle and fell back into the car.

Adam's gun came up.

Ian threw himself against Shannon, once more acting as her human shield.

Adam swore and yanked his gun down.

"Go." Ian's order came out a pained grunt, but must have gotten the message across.

The car took off, the momentum slamming the passenger door shut. Ian couldn't hold on and rolled back the other way, crunching his ruined arm between his body and the door before managing to twist around and fall back into the seat. His garbled curses were the last thing he heard before surrendering to the darkness.

Chapter Three

Shannon slammed the brakes, bringing the Charger to a bouncing stop in front of the emergency room doors. Muffled cursing had her wincing and looking at Ian. His normally handsome, chiseled features were almost unrecognizable beneath his blood-matted black-and-blond hair. He was slumped in the passenger seat, cradling his left arm against his abdomen, his deep blue eyes glazed with pain.

"We're here." She grabbed the massive revolver from the console and hid it in her purse just as a man in green scrubs ran out the sliding doors, motioning for her to move.

"Lady, you can't park here. This is the ambulance entrance. We've got one on the way, five minutes out."

"I need help!" she yelled through the open passenger window. "This man, he's hurt. I... found him a couple of blocks away, lying in

the street. I think he got mugged or something. His left arm may be broken."

Ian grunted, the corner of his swollen
mouth lifting in a half grin as he nodded. He
approved of her lies. No surprise there. She
was good at lying, had been doing it most of
her life just to survive.

The man in scrubs leaned in, his eyes going
wide when he saw Ian. He turned and motioned toward the doors to someone Shannon
couldn't see. A moment later another man in
scrubs ran outside, pushing a wheelchair at
a run.

"Sir, I'm Nurse Jack. I'm going to help you.
Can you tell me what happened?" The first
man eased open the door and crouched inside,
checking Ian's injuries.

For some reason, the nurse's name seemed
to amuse Ian. He chuckled and mumbled
something that sounded oddly like "Sparrow."

"What's his name?" Jack asked.

"I'm not sure. He mumbled *Ian*, I think."

Ian gave her a thumbs-up, acting loopy. He
never acted loopy. Just what had that jerk at
the truck stop done to him?

The two men struggled to lift Ian out of
the car. But they managed to get him into
the wheelchair without dumping him onto
the concrete. The second one took off, push-

ing Ian toward the emergency room doors. Jack shut the car door and crouched by the window, motioning toward the parking lot to Shannon's left.

"Park over there and come inside. We've got policemen here 24/7. One of them will want to take your statement."

"Of course. Be right in. Thank you so much for your help."

He gave her a tight, suspicious smile. "We don't see enough Good Samaritans these days. That guy owes you. Thanks." He backed up to the curb.

Feeling like the fraud she was, she smiled back, then pulled Ian's car into the lot. With Nurse Jack watching, she parked in the first spot she came to, halfway down the row. She stalled for time by rolling up the windows one at a time. Then she grabbed her purse and cut the engine before slowly getting out of the car.

She could feel Jack watching her, so she kept up the charade. She smoothed her T-shirt over her jeans and strolled toward the emergency room.

Giving up his vigil, he jogged back to the hospital, convinced that his Good Samaritan was coming inside to talk to the police as instructed.

Like *that* would ever happen.

She ducked down the next row of cars, then took off running in the opposite direction. The next two hours were spent shuffling between fast-food restaurants and convenience stores, all within a few blocks of the hospital. Every time she stayed in one place long enough to start getting curious stares, she'd switch locations and start over.

Now, standing outside the ER once again, she debated the wisdom of going inside. Had she waited long enough to avoid the cops? Were they looking for her? What about Ian? Where was he? There was no way to know whether the doctors had already patched up his injuries. Emergency rooms were notorious for long waits. But he'd been in rough shape. Surely they would have taken care of him by now.

As she cautiously approached, she kept an eye out for Nurse Jack and the man who'd wheeled Ian into the emergency room. When she didn't see either one, she straightened her shoulders and marched inside. One of the things that Ian had taught her since moving into the other side of the duplex that she rented was to hide in plain sight. Most people wouldn't question a person's right to be somewhere if they acted with confidence, pretending they belonged. Proving the point, no one stopped her or questioned her as she moved through the maze of rooms, gleaning bits of information left for anyone to take if they paid attention.

Like the sign-in sheet at the triage desk when the nurse turned away to talk to someone.

And the whiteboard with patient numbers instead of names, but with medical descriptions beside them: *flu-like symptoms, fever, possible dislocated or fractured arm.*

That dislocation or fracture could be Ian. Nothing else on the board fit. It still shocked her that he'd lost the fight so easily. She'd seen him take on four guys a few days ago outside their duplex because he was incensed that they were selling weed to the neighborhood kids. Those guys had left bleeding and bruised with their drugs confiscated. Ian had come away relatively unscathed. So how had he been beaten up by one lone man?

True, the guy was brawny and a few inches taller than Ian. But his shoulders weren't as broad, his arms not as ripped. Normally Ian fought like a junkyard dog, scrappy and vicious, holding nothing back. Today he'd seemed sluggish. It didn't make sense.

After a few more minutes of snooping and some unauthorized trips into areas off-limits to patients, she had a room number. He'd been taken to the fifth floor half an hour ago. From what she could understand from the medical jargon she'd sneaked and read, he'd been lucky. His arm was deeply bruised and sprained, dislocated and rotated back into place, but not broken. He did have a minor concussion. No surprise there. And he also had bruised ribs. Again, he was lucky they weren't broken. The blood he'd been coughing up had come from a cut on the inside of his cheek. He'd be in a lot of pain for a few days. But at least he was going to be okay, or so she hoped. She wanted to see him for herself to be sure.

Ducking out of a restricted area into the main hallway, she swept her gaze back and forth, on the lookout for Nurse Jack or the cops he'd mentioned. The elevators were a little farther down. She just might make it. Then she'd find out if Ian was okay, and whether he'd been able to discover anything about Maria before that stupid bully had interfered.

She scanned the intersecting hallway just before the ladies' room and the bank of elevators, then froze. Three impressively muscled, tall, dark-haired men in business suits were striding down the hall toward her. The one in the middle was half-turned, talking to the man on his right. He had the slightest limp, barely noticeable, as if his left leg bothered him. She'd seen that limp before. And she'd seen that profile, at the truck stop.

He was the man who'd beaten Ian.

She put on a burst of speed and ducked into the ladies' room. The door had just swung shut when footsteps echoed outside. Had he seen her? Recognized her? She waited, pressing a hand to her chest as if she could force her pulse to stop racing so fast.

A toilet flushed in one of the stalls. She started primping in the mirror, finger-combing her black hair to make the blue tips lie flat against her shoulders.

An older lady in a yellow sunflower-print dress stepped to a sink two down from her, smiling politely even though her disapproving gaze shot to the tattoos on Shannon's arms.

She'd probably faint if she saw the ones on her back.

Shannon hid a smile and grabbed a paper towel, pretending to dry her hands as she listened for sounds from the hallway. The footsteps had stopped. The elevator dinged. She tensed, her hand dropping to her purse, where the .357 rested inside. As soon as the elevator dinged again, she peeked out the door. The men were gone. She rushed into the hallway to the elevators. Only one was moving, the digital numbers above it marking its ascent.

Two. Three.

Keep going. Keep going.

Four.

Don't stop, don't stop.

Five. The elevator stopped.

Her stomach sank. The man who'd attacked Ian and possibly wrecked their plans to finally rescue Maria had somehow figured out where he was.

And he'd brought reinforcements.

Chapter Four

Ian awkwardly shifted against the pillows in his hospital bed as he clutched the phone to his right ear. While he listened to his boss, he watched the door at the other end of the room. He'd managed to keep his true identity a secret from the doctors and nurses so far. He aimed to keep it that way, at least until he discovered whether his cover had been blown with Butch.

"Did you get all that, Ian?"

"Yeah. Got it. Assistant District Attorney Cameron Ellison is a wuss. He wants me to drop my investigation. Doesn't mean I will."

A heavy sigh sounded in his ear. "We can't run roughshod over the locals. We have to play nice in their sandbox. And he's not asking us to drop it, just put it on hold for a few days, let things cool off. There were complaints at the truck stop. Several people saw the fight and called it in. That kind of exposure doesn't help any of us."

Ian's hand tightened around the phone so hard his knuckles ached. "If those same people paid attention to the *real* trouble going on around them, maybe we wouldn't have this human trafficking epidemic."

"Ian—"

"Please tell me you don't really expect me to back off. What do you think is going to happen to those girls if I do? I'm pretty sure I told you about ten of them were kids. We're talking thirteen, fourteen, *maybe*. And two of them, my God, Nash. They were children. Little kids. We can't sit on this. Don't ask me to do that. I won't. I *can't*."

Another sigh sounded through the phone. "What do you think you can do at this point? They saw you with Adam. They either suspect or know you're in law enforcement."

"Maybe, maybe not. They don't know for sure what Adam does. Butch just got the cop vibe from him is all. And they wouldn't expect a cop to pick a fight with another cop the way I did. There's plenty of doubt there. I can build on that."

"And how do you propose to do that?"

"I go back to work, back to the shop. Stick

to my routine. If they still want a deal, Wolverine will contact me again."

"And if they think you tried to set them up, they may try to kill you."

"It wouldn't be the first time someone tried to finish me off, and I'm still here. Nash, come on. Let me do this. Give me one more chance to set the trap and catch these slimeballs. For the love of all that's holy, help me get those little kids back to their parents." The phone went silent. "Boss, you still there?"

"I'm here."

"What's it gonna be? Let some local prosecutor call the shots and sacrifice dozens of young victims? Or do I get to wrap this thing up and make a difference for once?"

"You've rescued hundreds of victims since becoming an agent. You're making a difference."

"Doesn't feel that way from where I'm sitting. I've spent months building my cover, getting that noxious Wolverine kid to trust me. We're almost at the end. You pull me out now and bring someone else in, it'll take them months, longer, to get back to this point. Maybe you end up with a prosecutable case. Maybe you don't. Either way, it doesn't help the victims we know are in or near Gatlinburg right this minute. Rescuing those in need comes before prosecution. That's how we've always done things. A victim-centered approach. Or did our charter change while I was unconscious?"

"You know dang well it didn't. Fine, fine. You win. Based on those photographs, we know there are approximately thirty victims in jeopardy—"

"Thirty-two. He mentioned two Latina women."

"All right. Thirty-two. You and I both know how fast this scum likes to move their inventory, especially around a hub like you've discovered out here. If you've still got this Butch guy interested, maybe he'll wait and give you one more chance. Forty-eight hours, Ian. That's all I can give you. After that, we do it ADA Ellison's way. Might as well try to put someone in prison after all these months even if we don't end up rescuing the victims."

He hated that his boss was right. If he didn't make a deal in the next day or two, the victims were likely beyond their reach, already sold to the highest bidder. Bringing down the trafficking ring would be the only way to prevent others from becoming future victims. But he wasn't giving up on the girls he'd seen in those pictures. *The children.* Not yet. Someone had to fight for them. It might as well be him.

"All right. Forty-eight hours. I still get Chris as my contact? Same signals, same setup? I don't have time to train someone else, establish new parameters and routines."

"Nothing's changed from my perspective. It's the scum you've been dealing with who may feel otherwise. If they even suspect who you really are—"

"They don't."

"Can you guarantee that?"

Ian's mouth tightened. What could he say? He had no way of knowing for sure what Butch suspected, or didn't suspect.

"I didn't think so," Nash said. "I'm adding a condition to your forty-eight hours. Every time you go out, you put on Kevlar."

"Boss—"

"Nonnegotiable. Either wear the vest, or I shut this operation down right now."

Ian swore. Kevlar added risk, especially with his contacts possibly spooked. But if something did happen, and he wasn't wearing his vest and somehow survived—Nash would can him in a second. Then what would Ian do? This wasn't just his career. It was his life. There wasn't anything else.

Shannon. There was still Shannon.

He shook his head. Stupid dreams. There was no possibility of a future between the two of them. She thought he was simply the mechanic who lived on the other side of her duplex. Once she found out he was in law enforcement, he'd become enemy number one. He'd never see her again.

Of all the people he'd duped in his career, Shannon was the one he truly regretted. She wasn't some criminal or thug. She was a genuinely good person, a survivor. She'd worked so hard trying to find her friend Maria, who was still trapped in the life that Shannon had escaped. That story had been shared with Ian over dinner and a few too many glasses of wine one night. It had also been the catalyst that had sent his investigation in an entirely new direction.

What Shannon told him about believing Maria might be in the area had eventually led him to Wolverine. She was a hero, and didn't even know it. She trusted him, thinking he wanted to help her find her friend, because of the attraction they shared and because he was a good person.

He hadn't faked the attraction.

But the guilt was eating him alive that he'd misled her about his motives, that everything else he'd told her was a lie. Almost. In order to gain her trust, he'd revealed his own extremely personal dark secret, a secret he'd never told anyone else. Which only went to show how obsessed he was with this case, or with Shannon. He'd always planned on taking that particular secret with him to the grave.

"Ian? You still there?"

He shook his head again, then winced when the movement jump-started the headache that had been threatening since the fight with Adam. Maybe he could bum an aspirin or something stronger off a nurse before escaping this place. "I'm here."

"What about the vest? Do we have a deal?"

He blinked against the bright fluorescent lights overhead and longed to rub his aching temples. But with his left hand in a sling and the phone in his right, all he could do was squeeze his eyes shut. "We have a deal. My vest is at the duplex. I'll put it on before I head to the shop in the morning."

"You'd better. If these guys decide they can't trust you, that vest is your only chance. First sign of trouble, use the nuclear option. I'll have the cavalry in place to come running. Understood?"

The nuclear option meant blowing his cover, sending the signal for agent in distress. It would activate every asset in the area to come help him. But it would ruin his chances of rescuing anyone. He had no intention of using it. Ever.

"Understood." Technically, he hadn't made a promise. "What about the ADA?"

"Leave him to me. I'll tell him you're lying low, letting things settle. Don't make me regret this, Ian. Be careful. See if you can figure out the location of the victims so we can set up a rescue operation. Then shut it down. Don't try to be a hero and get yourself killed. The paperwork would be a nightmare."

Ian laughed, then winced at the sharp jolt that shot through his cut cheek. His stomach clenched. The pain was making him nauseous.

"Ian?"

"Okay, okay. I'll do what I can to keep you from all that paperwork. You're going to pick up the hospital tab, right? My crappy car mechanic insurance won't cover an ER visit without a hefty deductible."

"I'll take care of it." The line clicked.

Chapter Five

Ian dumped the landline phone onto the side table and clutched his aching head. But he couldn't allow himself the luxury of sitting there until the pain receded. He needed to leave. Now.

He stood, then had to grab the bed railing to keep from falling. When the room stopped spinning, he hobbled to the bathroom and splashed water on his face. A few deep breaths seemed to help with the nausea. He cupped his hands beneath the faucet and drank some water. Then, seeing the blood smeared on his face and matting his hair, he did a quick wash in the sink. Finally, looking more presentable and feeling less shaky, he went on a hunt for his clothes.

A few minutes and several curses later, he was fully dressed, minus his favorite leather jacket. It had died a tragic death beneath the scissors of a nurse trying to work it off his injured arm. It would have come in handy right now to hide the splotches of blood on his shirt. But he figured that was to be expected in a hospital. People would just assume it was someone else's blood, that he'd helped a friend into the emergency room. He couldn't imagine anyone would try to stop him, as long as he made sure the nurse assigned to him didn't see him leaving the room.

He still felt naked without a gun. Shannon had his .357 Magnum and his car, which meant she presumably had his Glock .22 pistol, as well. Thankfully, his house key and wallet were in his jeans pocket, so he'd be able to hire a car to drive him home. And he wouldn't have to kick in the door when he got there. Bonus. That was one tiny bright spot in what had turned into a wasted day.

The second bright spot was that Shannon hadn't gotten hurt. When she'd pulled that gun on Adam, Ian had been terrified that she'd get killed. Hopefully, she'd gone home and was lying low. He didn't think Butch or the others had seen her rescuing him at the end of the fight. The van had been gone by then. But he wanted her away from any potential danger, just in case.

He never should have taken her to that truck stop with him, even if it meant rescheduling the meeting. He should have ignored her impassioned pleas that he not delay, that he go directly to the rendezvous point. He shouldn't have believed her promises that she'd stay in the car and wouldn't interfere.

Then again, she *had* stayed in the car.

He grinned at the memory of her daring to call Adam a bully. The woman was just as feisty as she was gorgeous. But knowing Adam, he probably had a BOLO out on her *and* Ian, just on principle. Every cop in Gatlinburg, Tennessee, had likely been alerted to be on the lookout for the two of them. Which meant if they saw her, especially driving the Charger Adam had seen, she'd be handcuffed and thrown in jail.

In the few months that Ian had known her, one thing was clear—she had a deep-seated fear of law enforcement. If she ended up under arrest, the second she made bail she'd run. He'd never see her again. That shouldn't matter. But it did.

He was halfway to the door when it started to open. He was mentally spinning a cover story to explain why he was dressed and walking when the nurse stepped inside. Except it wasn't a nurse. And it wasn't just one person. It was three.

Adam was flanked by Duncan and Colin.

And they were looking at him as if they thought he was the slime stuck to the bottom of their shoes. Nothing had changed since the last time they'd all seen each other. When was that? Probably last Easter, a good seven months ago. Not nearly long enough.

"Where do you think you're going?" Adam stepped in front of him, blocking his way.

Ian braced his legs and fisted his right hand at his side, fully expecting all three of them to take a turn trying to wallop him. One-on-one, even though each of them was a tad bigger than him, he'd normally have at least a fifty-fifty chance. But he wasn't exactly at his best tonight. Still, he'd give it a good solid try if they pushed him. As ticked off as he was about this truly screwed-up day, it could give him the advantage.

"If you're here for round two, Adam, be warned that I'm not throwing the fight this time. You're the one who'll be bleeding on the floor when we're through."

"I knew it," Adam said. "You were pulling punches at the truck stop. I figured it was either that or you'd gone soft. Why did you pick the fight to begin with? And what in the world were you doing with those losers by that van?"

He shrugged, then pressed his hand against

his protesting ribs. "Losers hang with losers, right?" The other two were intently watching him, but seemed content to let Adam do the talking for this little welcoming committee. "I'd love to reminisce about old times with you boys, but I have things that need doing."

He stepped around Adam. As one, Colin and Duncan moved to block him, spreading their legs and bracing themselves against whatever he might try.

He blew out a deep breath. "So that's how it's going to be, huh? You can't butt out and let it lie? Fine. There's still some fight left in me. But to be fair, let's do this one at a time." He motioned toward the sling on his left arm. "Just to even the odds."

"Knock off the sarcasm." Adam crossed his arms, his brow knitting into a frown.

"Who's being sarcastic? I can take you guys." He motioned toward Adam. "You first. Payback time."

He rolled his eyes, unimpressed. "What did the doctors say was wrong? Do you have broken ribs? A concussion? They don't typically admit someone for a broken arm."

"What do you care?"

Colin shoved him. "Knock it off, Ian. What's really going on? Adam told us about those pieces of scum that you were with at the truck stop. Associating with guys like that is low, even for you."

"Even for me? Gee, thanks, Colin. That makes me feel all warm and fuzzy inside. Can't wait to see what you write on my next Christmas card." He tried to shove him out of his way.

Colin shoved right back.

"Leave him alone," a feminine voice called out from behind the Colin-Duncan wall.

Ian groaned as Colin and Duncan turned around. Shannon stood just inside the door, holding his .357 Magnum revolver in both her hands.

In the blink of an eye, three pistols were pointing directly at her.

"Drop it," Adam ordered. "Now."

Her face turned chalk white. Her arms started to shake.

Ian moved between Colin and Shannon, once again playing human shield. He was really getting tired of that role. "Guys, dial it back. Shannon, give me the gun."

"But they were—"

"It's okay. Trust me. Please." He held out his hand.

She hesitated, her hands shaking dangerously, her finger on the trigger.

He purposely kept his voice gentle and

calming as he spoke. "Shannon, darlin', I really need you to move your finger off the trigger and give me the gun. You think you can do that?"

Her blue-tipped black bangs had fallen into her eyes. She tossed her head, green eyes darting back and forth from the others to him. None of them had lowered their weapons. They'd simply shifted their stances so they could aim at her without him in the line of fire. They wouldn't shoot him. But they didn't know Shannon and weren't taking any chances with her.

"Shannon—"

"Okay, okay." She moved her finger off the trigger and turned the gun around.

He blew out a relieved breath as he took the gun. "Thank you. You did great." He smiled encouragingly and shoved the revolver into his jeans pocket.

The others lowered their weapons and slowly put them away, as if they were worried that she might draw another gun.

Ian turned sideways so he could keep an eye on all of them. He smiled at Shannon again and motioned to the others. "Shannon Murphy, allow me to introduce you to the brute I allowed to beat the crap out of me at the truck stop. This is Adam McKenzie, a law enforcement ranger for the National Park Service."

Adam nodded, but maintained a tense watchful wariness.

Shannon's eyes widened, panic welling in them as soon as she'd heard the words *law enforcement*. He rushed through the rest of the introductions.

"The second one who looks like he could be Adam's twin, but isn't, is Special Agent Duncan McKenzie, also with NPS. Our last black-haired blue-eyed Irish lad is Deputy US Marshal Colin McKenzie."

She swallowed, her haunted eyes zeroing in on him. "Why are they here, Ian? And why do they look so much like *you*?"

The knowledge was in her eyes. But she obviously needed to hear him admit it before she'd accept what to her was likely an unforgivable deception. He thought about lying. But there'd been enough lies between them already. And he knew the others wouldn't go along with whatever story he wove, not without understanding *why*. All he could do was hope the fragile bond that he and Shannon had formed over the past few months survived the next few minutes.

"They're here because they're my brothers."

She swallowed again, twisting her hands together. "I'm guessing that Ian Savage isn't your real name. And you're not really a mechanic?"

He glanced at his brothers, who were watching the conversation with riveted interest, before he met her tortured gaze again.

"I *am* a mechanic. I can fix pretty much anything with an engine. But I only work at the shop as my cover while working a case. My real name is Ian *McKenzie*. I'm a special agent for Homeland Security, specializing in the fight against human trafficking."

A sob burst from her lips and she ran from the room.

Colin started after her, yanking open the door to give chase.

Ian grabbed his arm. "Let her go. She's terrified of anyone with a badge. For good reason."

Colin hesitated, then let the door close. "Special agent with Homeland Security, huh?" His voice was heavy with disbelief. "Since when?"

"Ian *Savage*?" Duncan cocked his head and grinned. "What a lame cover name." He winked, letting Ian know he was teasing.

Normally Ian didn't get Duncan's jokes or appreciate the lighthearted way he approached life. But at this moment, he was Ian's favorite brother.

"Let's hold the twenty questions until Ian's back in bed." Adam firmly grasped his shoulders and steered him farther into the room.

"I must have hit you harder than I thought," Ian mused. "You're limping."

"Old injury. You don't get any credit for that. Come on. You're about ready to fall over."

"I'm only going to lie down because there's no point in leaving now. You'll just follow me and badger me with questions."

Adam chuckled. "Right. It has nothing to do with how wobbly you are or that you look like you're about to pass out."

Ian stopped beside the bed. "You forgot something else."

"What's that?"

"I'm also about to throw up."

Adam's eyes widened. He jumped back just as Ian lost the contents of his stomach on the floor.

Chapter Six

"*Four years*, Ian?" Adam's brows drew down in a thunderous frown as he dried his hands in the bathroom doorway. While he'd cleaned the floor moments earlier, and his shoes, the others had dragged extra chairs into the room. Now, as Adam took a seat, he and the others formed a ring around the bed, effectively boxing Ian in as if to keep him from trying to leave again.

"You must have gone to college after taking off and never told anyone about it. Then you joined Homeland Security shortly after you graduated."

"Your deductive reasoning and math skills are extraordinary. You're wasting your talents as a ranger."

Adam's eyes narrowed dangerously.

Colin swore. "Why all the subterfuge? We see you once, twice a year if that. And every time we ask about your life, you give a different story about your occupation. One time you were a bartender. Once you were a taxi driver in New York."

"Don't forget cowboy on a dude ranch in Montana," Duncan chimed in. "That was my favorite." He motioned toward Ian's neck and arms. "Those tats real?"

"Why all the lies?" Colin demanded.

"I didn't lie. I *was* all those things. And, yes, Duncan, the tattoos are real."

Duncan waved toward his hair. "The blond streaks are new. Can't say I care for them."

Ian shot him an aggravated look. "Can't say I care about your opinion."

Duncan grinned.

Colin frowned. "Those were never real jobs. They were cover for whatever you were doing for Homeland Security." He waved toward the other two. "It's not like we can't relate. We've all done undercover work. And we're brothers in blue in addition to blood. We would have kept your secrets, been there for you over the years instead of—"

"Instead of judging me and telling me what a screwup I was all the time?" Ian started to cross his arms, but the sling stopped him. "Thanks, but no thanks. I got enough of that from all of you—and Dad—while growing up."

Adam fisted his hand on top of the bed railing to Ian's right. "That's not fair. You *were* a screwup back in those days. You vandalized houses, stole cars, did drugs. All we ever did was try to help you."

"Uh, no. You beat the crap out of me and tattled to Mom and Dad. And for the record, I've never done drugs. Not even while undercover."

Adam rolled his eyes. "What are we? Ten? Let's talk about this like grown adults. Or if we can't do that, let's speak to each other as the professionals that we are. Ian, if you're in some kind of trouble, we can help."

Ian snorted. "Of course you'd think I was in trouble."

"Stop it." This time it was Duncan who spoke up, sounding serious for a change. "I don't think Adam was saying that on a personal level. He meant on whatever case you're working. You told that girl—"

"Shannon."

"Right. Shannon. You told her that you were working as a mechanic as your cover. That you specialize in fighting human trafficking. Is that why you're in town? You're after a trafficking ring? Where does Shannon Murphy fit into that? Who is she?"

Adam tapped the railing. "And what does it all have to do with Butch Gillespie? Has he risen from common pimp to running modern slavery rings?"

Ian straightened, then sucked in a breath and rubbed his aching ribs. "Gillespie? That's his last name? You know him?"

"When I was a Memphis cop, I worked on numerous task forces. That included vice, specifically prostitution. Gillespie was arrested during one of our raids. The net was wide, mostly circumstantial evidence. He was one of the fish who got away. Not enough to hold him beyond the first twenty-four hours. No one was willing to turn on him, make any deals. He walked. But there's no doubt in my mind that he was one of the ones behind the ring we broke up."

"When was that?" Ian asked.

Adam considered it a moment. "Two, maybe two and a half years ago."

"What did you find out about him? Did he run with anyone called Axel or Jagger?"

"Not that I remember. His right-hand guys went to prison. No way they're out already. Are Axel and Jagger the other two big guys who were leaning against that van when I saw you?"

Ian nodded. "My thug contact, the scrawny guy by the front bumper, finally got me a face-to-face meeting after I'd been trying to talk deals for weeks using him as an intermediary. I'd hoped to make the bust tonight, rescue dozens of girls and bring down a major trafficking hub right here in Gatlinburg."

Adam held his hands out. "Sorry, man. I had no way of knowing you were working a case. I didn't even know you were in town. Maybe if you'd told us that you had—"

"Don't," Ian warned.

Adam let out a deep breath. "No judgment, all right? I'm just saying that had I known you were a special agent with Homeland Security, I wouldn't have interfered. As for Gillespie, if you want, I can call some of my guys in Memphis and have them email me what they've got on him."

Ian stared at him in surprise. "O…kay. Sure. I'd appreciate that."

"You don't have to act so shocked. We're brothers, in and out of uniform. I'm always here for you, Ian. We all are."

Duncan and Colin nodded as if on cue.

Ian was so used to being on the defensive around his family that he wasn't sure how to react to this new uneasy truce, of sorts. He finally nodded his thanks, hoping that was enough.

Duncan thumped the railing. "Homeland Security, huh? Impressive. Tell us about it."

It was surreal sitting in the hospital bed chatting with his brothers. That never happened. Since leaving home at eighteen, his return visits had been short and more for his mom than anyone else. He'd never once considered that the others might really care about him. Or did they?

After giving them a small glimpse into the kind of work he did, he said, "Tell me the truth. If I wasn't in law enforcement, would you even be talking to me right now?"

Duncan considered the question, then rested his forearms on the railing. "Probably not. Your turn. If you weren't still woozy and thought you could get past the three of us, would you still be here?"

He reluctantly smiled. "Probably not."

Duncan grinned. "Back to your current case. You working alone?"

"Except for a liaison agent I meet at a pizza parlor every now and then so he can update my boss and provide resources, it's just me. I've spent months following dozens of tips and leads through three states. Everything pointed to Gatlinburg being a hub, a distribution point. We've made some minor busts along the way. But here in Tennessee, I'm hoping to bring it all to a head. I want Butch and his men in handcuffs. But mostly I want to rescue the girls he's currently holding. Unfortunately, I haven't figured out where he's keeping them or I'd have gotten them out by now."

"I'm so sorry," Adam repeated. "I had no idea about the damage I was doing when I confronted you in that parking lot."

"Do you realize that's the first time you've ever apologized to me?"

Adam snorted. "It's the first time you ever deserved it."

Ian's jaw tightened.

"That was a joke. Not a good one, but an attempt regardless." Adam smiled, but his look was wary. "I'm not Duncan. I don't have the silly gene."

"Hey, hey. Duncan's in the room here, guys," Duncan said.

Adam arched a brow. "Insulting you wouldn't be any fun if you weren't."

Duncan grinned. "There's hope for you yet, my serious brother."

Adam rolled his eyes. "What's your number, Ian? I'll text you once I hear back from Memphis PD about Gillespie." He pulled out his phone.

Ian hesitated.

Adam arched a brow. "What am I supposed to do? Shine the bat signal and hope you see it?"

The weight of all three brothers' stares focused on him. Did they think that this civil conversation meant all was forgiven? That they could suddenly be friends? When they thought he was Ian the rebel, Ian the delinquent, they wanted nothing to do with him. But now that they knew he'd followed the family tradition of going into law enforcement after all, they suddenly wanted to be cozy?

Screw that.

They might consider everything that had happened as water under the McKenzie family bridge, but he wasn't ready to throw out an olive branch. Especially since he hadn't taken this job to make their retired-judge father proud. He'd taken it *in spite* of his father, to right the terrible wrong that Mighty McKenzie had done so many years ago. Not that anything could ever atone for what he'd done.

For what Ian *hadn't* done, but *should* have done.

He rattled off a number and waited until Adam had saved it in his contacts. "That's my boss's line. His name is Barry Nash. You can text him about the case file on Gillespie. He'll see that I get the information."

Adam jerked his head up. "You gave me your boss's number?"

"It's the best I can do right now without risking blowing my cover. I don't have an electronic trail in my real name here in town. I'm Ian Savage. Period. Mostly I use burner phones."

Adam gave him a resigned look. "All right."

Surprised at how easily his oldest brother had given in, Ian thanked him. "I appreciate you accepting my decision."

"Oh, I'm not accepting it. I respect that you don't want us interfering in an investigation. But now that we've found you again, I have no intention of letting you disappear like you usually do. Things are different now, Ian." He held up his left hand. A gold band winked in the overhead lights.

"What the— You got hitched?"

"Last June. And both Colin and Duncan are engaged. They're tying the knots in a double ceremony this Christmas. Are you going to miss every important moment in our lives because of your silly grievances against Dad and your resentment at us for not hating him like you do? Or are you going to finally grow up and work through whatever made you leave all those years ago?"

"Get out."

Adam blinked. "Excuse me?"

"Get out. Forget about Gillespie. I'll get the information myself. Forget about me and my *silly grievances*. I never asked for this little reunion, and I have no intention of *growing up* anytime soon." He pushed the call button on the side of the bed.

Colin put his hand on Adam's shoulder. "Come on. He's not ready. We'll come back later."

"What exactly do you think Dad did?" Adam demanded.

"Nurse's station." A woman's voice crackled through the speaker built into the bed railing.

"I have some guests who've overstayed their welcome," Ian told her. "They don't seem inclined to leave on their own."

"Do you need me to call security, Mr. Savage?"

Ian arched a brow.

Adam swore. "This isn't over." He stood, jerked his suit jacket into place and strode to the door. Colin followed without a backward glance. Duncan gave Ian a sad smile and exited with them.

"Mr. Savage?" the nurse called out again.

"Never mind. They've left now. Thank you."

He wrestled down the bed railing that Adam had raised after Ian had nearly thrown up on him. He swung his legs over the side and used the bedside phone to call Shannon's cell. No answer. He left her a message, then called his own cell in case she'd answer that.

She didn't. For a day that had started out so promising, it was turning out to be one of the worst ones ever. And he'd had more than his share of bad days in his twenty-seven years.

Less than five minutes later, he walked out the emergency room doors without anyone trying to stop him. Not wanting to risk his brothers seeing him if they were still hanging around the hospital, he'd phoned for a car for hire to pick him up a few blocks away.

He was halfway through the parking lot to the agreed pickup place when he spotted a familiar black Charger parked in one of the spots. *His* black Charger. He hurried toward it, half expecting to see Shannon waiting there. His shoulders slumped with disappointment when he saw it was empty. He'd stupidly hoped she might have come back to give him a chance to explain. Where was she? Had she hired someone to drive her home, as he'd planned for himself? Maybe she'd left a note inside the car.

He'd just unlocked the door when tires screeched behind him. He turned to see an all-too-familiar white panel van, idling behind the Charger.

Ah, hell.

He kept his expression bland and nodded at Butch, who was driving. "I was going to call you to reschedule our meeting since we were rudely interrupted."

"I'll just bet you were, *cop*."

The side door slid open to reveal Blade aiming a sawed-off shotgun at him. "Get in."

Chapter Seven

Shannon strode toward the emergency room exit. She'd debated taking Ian's car when she ran from his hospital room. After all, he'd lied to her all this time. He deserved to be stranded when they discharged him, forced to figure out his own way to get home. Maybe he could ask one of his brothers for help.

Brothers.

He'd told her he didn't have any family. He was an orphan, grew up in foster care. And those were just a few of his lies. Had anything he'd said been true? Had the make-out sessions on his couch been real? Or was that some kind of cover for a reason that she hadn't figured out yet?

She clenched her fists and moved back to allow a gurney to roll past. Just thinking about how badly she'd been duped, and used, had her lungs squeezing in her chest. Had he been laughing at her this whole time? Pretending to commiserate with her, pretending to be her friend? Why? Why had he done it?

She shook her head. Didn't matter. They were done. Over. All the silly fantasies she'd had that their fledgling relationship might turn into something deeper, that maybe she'd finally found someone who *got* her, who didn't judge her for her past, had died the moment he'd introduced himself as a cop.

Ian Savage, a cop. No, Ian *McKenzie*. Brother of three other cops. Or special agents. Or investigators. Or whatever they were. None of it computed. None of it mattered.

Not anymore.

He deserved to be stranded at the hospital. She didn't trust him now any more than she did the strangers in his room, those men who'd looked so much like him that her heart had broken the moment they'd turned around. She'd known, immediately upon seeing them shoulder to shoulder with Ian, that they were all brothers. She'd known Ian had lied to her about being an orphan. And then it had only gotten worse.

Still, she couldn't quite bring herself to steal his car when his arm was in a sling and he had a concussion. Stupid, yes. But there it was. She was a sucker and felt sorry for him even though he didn't deserve her sympathy.

But just because he was a jerk didn't mean she had to stoop to his level. His phone and pistol were already hidden inside the car. All she had to do was leave the key under the mat and walk away.

She'd hire a car to pick her up at one of the fast-food restaurants close by. Hanging around the hospital any longer than she already had was too risky. She'd wasted half an hour hiding out, walking the halls, worried he or his brothers were after her. Now she had to get home and pack. It wouldn't take long. She never set roots down very deep. Most of her stuff she could put into one suitcase. The duplex she rented came mostly furnished. What few pieces of furniture she'd added weren't worth taking.

The emergency room doors slid open. She'd just reached the end of the row where she'd left his car when she realized a white van was parked behind it. A familiar-looking man dressed in black straightened beside the Charger, slammed the passenger door and shoved something into his pocket. Then he ran to the van and hopped inside. It took off, tires squealing, and turned down another row as the side door slid shut.

But not before she saw Ian inside, with one

of the thugs from the truck stop pointing a shotgun at him.

She took off running toward the Charger.

Risking her life to help him made no sense, except that in spite of the lies, he'd helped her a dozen times since they'd first met—from loaning her grocery money when unexpected expenses ate into her emergency fund to fixing her car for free. No matter how betrayed she felt, she couldn't do nothing and just let him be murdered. Even the idea of him being hurt squeezed her heart. She'd begun to fall for him, and it was going to be frustratingly hard undoing that mistake. Meanwhile, she had to help him, if she could just figure out how.

She watched the van make a right turn out of the parking lot as she grabbed the car key from her jeans pocket. *Hurry, hurry, hurry.*

She shoved the key in the door lock.

The van stopped at the light three blocks down.

A hand clamped down on her shoulder. She whirled, fist drawn back, ready to let it fly.

The man swore and grabbed both her arms before she could throw the punch. "Why are you trying to run me over, shoot me or hit me every time I see you?"

She blinked and looked up into the face of one of Ian's brothers. Adam, the one from the truck stop. Cop. He was a cop. She started to shake. *Ian, what about Ian?* She looked over her shoulder. The white van was gone. Where was it? She scanned the road.

"It's Shannon Murphy, right? I'll let you go if you promise not to try to coldcock me again."

There. The van turned right at the next light. She jerked back toward Ian's brother. "Adam, right? You're the ranger, with the National Park Service?"

He frowned and let her go. "That's right." He glanced at the car, then at the key in her hand. "Can we talk? About my brother? I have a few questions, and when I saw you, I thought you might—"

"Not now. I'm in a hurry." She flung the door open.

He grabbed her arm again. "Listen, lady. I can arrest you right now for assault and half a dozen other charges for pulling a gun on me twice today. I just want to ask you a few questions."

She jerked back toward the road. The van was gone. They were getting away. And she didn't know where it was going. She had to do something. Fast. But this man was a cop, or a ranger, whatever. Could she trust him?

"Shannon?"

He was Ian's brother, and his life was on the line right now. She'd just have to hope that mattered to him. "The guys from the truck stop, they were here, just now."

His eyes widened. His left hand went to his hip like a reflex even though the gun she knew he had was covered by his suit jacket. He was left-handed, like Ian. The thought made her heart squeeze again.

"Did they hurt you? Are you okay?"

She blinked, surprised that he'd bother to ask. "I'm fine. But Ian isn't."

His gaze whipped back to hers. "What do you mean?"

"I saw him, inside the van. One of Butch's men was pointing a shotgun at him as the door slid shut." She pointed down the street. "They turned right at the light. I don't know where they're taking him but—"

"Give me the key. I'll try to catch up to him. You can wait here and—"

She tossed him the key and then dove inside, rolling over the center console into the passenger seat.

He jumped into the driver's seat, glaring at her. But he didn't waste time arguing. His jaw was set in a grim line as he drove out of the parking lot, dodging other cars that honked their horns at them.

He raced down the street, skidding through an intersection against the light, barely squeaking past an oncoming car without getting hit. They were on a main road through town, but there was no sign of a white van.

"Look right. I'll look left," he said.

She craned her neck, searching every street they passed. Brake lights caught her eye on a side street. "There, there! They just turned left."

"Hold on."

She braced her arms against the dash as he did a one-eighty in the middle of the road. Other drivers squealed their brakes and honked again. He ignored them, slamming the accelerator, bumping over a curb before heading down the road she'd indicated.

Shannon swallowed hard and clicked the seat belt into place.

"Where did they turn? Where?" Adam demanded.

"Just up ahead, past that white house. There!"

He careened around the corner without even slowing down.

The white van was in front of them now, a good sixty or so yards ahead. But it was a narrow residential street with lots of parked cars. Adam couldn't let the Charger go full speed without risking hitting a car or running someone down if they happened to step into the road.

He tossed his phone in the console and told Shannon his passcode. "Hit the favorites button. My boss is the first number, Yeong Lee. Tell him I need backup, to get Gatlinburg PD to try to cut the van off ahead of us."

She grabbed the phone. The van turned again. "It just turned—"

"Right. Got it. Make the call."

Her skin itched and her fingers shook as she did as Adam had directed. Calling the police for help went against everything in her experience. She'd called them for help when she was much younger. Instead of believing her, instead of helping her, they'd slapped her in handcuffs and put her in jail. But she knew she was no match for the men in that van. Ian needed help, real help, not her.

She pitched the phone into the console. "He said he'd direct Gatlinburg PD to this area, and to call him back as soon as we have a location."

Several hair-raising turns later she straightened in her seat. The van made another right turn, so far ahead of them they could barely see it.

"We're losing them," Adam snarled. "These dang streets. Why do people park all over the road?" He dodged several cars, sped ahead, then had to bump up into a front yard to avoid an oncoming car. With so many parked cars it was like going down a one-way road, the wrong way.

They rounded a corner. There was no sign of the van.

Adam cursed and slowed, looking down each side street.

Shannon thought about the various turns the van had made. "Adam, speed up. Head to the third street on the right."

"You saw them?" He floored the gas and a few seconds later they raced around the corner onto the next street. "I don't see the van. You sure you saw them?"

She shook her head. "No. I didn't see them. But I know where they're going."

Chapter Eight

When the van finally pulled to a stop and the door slid open, Ian breathed a sigh of relief that he was still alive. That relief disappeared when he looked around and realized they were in his garage. That must have been why Jack insisted on taking his car keys at the hospital. He must have retrieved the garage remote control, planning to come here since Wolverine knew this was where mechanic Ian Savage lived. If Shannon was in her side of the duplex right now, then she was in a world of danger. If she came over, Butch's henchmen would eliminate her as a potential witness to whatever they had planned for Ian.

Please don't be home, Shannon. Please be safe somewhere else.

Butch appeared in front of the van's open sliding door, tossed the garage door opener and car key to the concrete floor and grinned. "Home sweet home, eh, *cop*?"

A spark of alarm shot through him, but he rolled his eyes. "I'm the furthest thing from a cop you can get. Are you thinking that Gatlinburg PD saw my black-and-blond hair and my tattoos and thought I'd fit right in?" He snorted. "Yep, that's it. They rushed right over to sign me up. Get real, man. What is this? A shakedown to see whether I'm legit?" He gave Jagger and Axel disgusted looks, trying not to sweat over them both aiming long guns at him from opposite sides of the van's interior. "My buyers aren't going to be happy with the delay because of your grandstanding."

Butch braced both hands on the open doorway. "I recognized that guy from the truck stop. He's a cop from Memphis. And you know what? You sure do look an awful lot like him."

"Really? That's why you're accusing me of being a pig? Because I look like another one? That's just messed up." He motioned toward the thug he'd likened to Captain Jack Sparrow. "This guy could be a stunt double for Johnny Depp. Why's he here with you instead of soaking in a pool in Hollywood with his brother Johnny?"

Butch frowned. "You said that cop slept with your girlfriend. You may not like each other, but he called you by name. And I happen to know he's one of them McKenzies, that family of law enforcement brothers. What's their dad's name? The Mighty McKenzie or something like that? He used to run this town, and his sons are all in law enforcement. Coincidentally, I heard one of them is named Ian. I figure you're either a cop or a special agent of some kind, *McKenzie*."

Ian bluffed like he'd never bluffed before, like his life depended on it—which it did.

"McKenzie?" He rolled his eyes again. "Dude, those guys are rich. Some wealthy grandpappy passed down a dozen companies to those spoiled jerks." He motioned to the garage. "You think even if I wanted to be a cop like those guys that I'd be living in this dump if I had millions in the bank? You've lost your ever-lovin' mind."

Butch narrowed his eyes suspiciously, but he looked less certain than before. "If you ain't one of 'em, how do you know that Adam guy?"

Ian snorted. "He was at a party along with me and dozens of other people last summer. Other than being introduced when I came in, that was it. Except for the fact that I saw him making out with my girl in the kitchen. I was too ticked off to do anything that night. I left the party, and my girl. Next time I saw him was at the truck stop. Heck, you know more about him than I do. I didn't even remember his name. Probably the only reason he remembers mine is because my ex-girlfriend cries out my name every time he screws her."

Blade surprised him by laughing. He sobered when Butch shot him an aggravated look.

Butch gestured toward Ian. "That's why he knew your name? A party?"

"A party with dozens of other people. Hell, man. We were all there for the same reason— good food, free booze and hot chicks. You tellin' me you know everyone who shows up at parties? Get real."

Continuing his bluff, he shoved Butch out of his way and hopped down from the van. The garage walls seemed to bow in and out, making him dizzy. He covered it by leaning down and scooping up the garage door opener and car key. He immediately regretted the movement when his ribs sent a slice of burning pain lancing through him. He took shallow breaths and shoved the opener into his pocket, all the while trying not to wince or reveal how dizzy he was. Showing weakness around these types of men could be fatal. He casually leaned against the side of the van as if he had no worries in the world while he waited for the garage to stop spinning around him.

"You about done with the twenty questions?" he demanded. "Or are we done here?"

Butch exchanged a long look with his men, but didn't say anything.

Hoping he'd be able to walk without falling, Ian pushed away from the van. "Thanks for the ride home, boys. But unless you want to pick up where we left off and let me place an order, I'd just as soon you get your butts out of my garage. Heck, even if you do want to take an order, forget it. I'm too disgusted to even want to do business with you. I'll find a shipment somewhere else." He took a step toward the door to the house.

"Hold it. Let's not be too hasty here. Maybe I jumped to some conclusions and shouldn't have."

"You think?" Ian stalked to the door that led into the duplex, mainly because he desperately needed to hold on to the railing to keep from falling down.

"Ian, wait."

He let out an exaggerated sigh and turned, still clutching the railing. "Unless you're giving me back my .357 that your guys stole from me in the van, we've got nothing left to discuss."

"It's a nice gun. I'll have to think about that."
Ian turned around.

"Hold up."

He slowly faced Butch again, forced to let go of the railing. Thankfully, the dizziness was fading now. "What?"

Butch motioned to his men, and they drew their guns back inside the van. Ian was careful not to let his relief show on his face.

Butch stopped in front of him and held up the stack of pictures he'd had earlier. But before Ian could reach for them, Butch shoved them back into his jacket pocket. "I'm not saying I'm willing to trust you just yet. But I'm on the fence enough not to blow your head off."

"Is there a point to this?"

"The point is that I'm going to give it a few days, think on this. And if I decide you truly aren't messing with me, I'll be in touch."

Ian shook his head. "You want to deal with me, a few days won't cut it. My guy wants a shipment to take with him out of the country in the next twenty-four hours. I don't have two days. I'll have to get my girls somewhere else." He motioned toward the street out front. "Go on. Get out of my garage."

The two of them stood toe to toe, each one trying to read the other. Ian hoped he wasn't overplaying his hand. Reading people was his thing, and he sensed that Butch wanted to make a deal. Maybe he was having trouble moving inventory and didn't have enough buyers at the ready. Ian was walking a fine line so he wouldn't seem overeager. And yet he needed to keep this creep interested, or the poor women and girls he had would end up being sold to someone else, someone who wasn't interested in helping them, or saving them.

"Tell you what, Savage." He threw out a price. "You pay that, and I'll give you every girl I got. This town's getting way too hot, and I'm ready to move on. What do you say?"

Ian sighed as if bored, and took a chance, knowing it might be his last. "What about the two Latinas you mentioned at the truck stop? I've gone to way too much trouble not to get something for myself out of all this. That is, if they're as sexy as you claim."

"All my girls are top choice," Butch snarled as if insulted. "But these Spanish chicks are older, like I told you. That a problem?"

"Depends. You got pictures?"

Butch pulled out his cell phone. "Not printed up. They pretty much cater to me and the boys. I hadn't planned on letting them go. But a change might not be bad, something fresh." He grinned.

Ian kept his expression carefully blank as he fantasized about wrapping his fingers around Butch's throat and squeezing.

Butch turned the phone around. "What do you think? Pretty enough for you?"

Ian's breath caught. Finally, after all this time. There she was: Maria. Had to be. The lighting in the picture was terrible. All he could see of their features were dark eyes and dark hair. But there was no mistaking the pink butterfly tattoo on the right side of one of the women's necks, just as Shannon had described.

Ian shrugged, acting as nonchalant as he could manage. "They'll do. And the price is good. You've got a deal. I'll need some time to get the money from my buyer and arrange a truck for transport." *And get both Homeland Security agents and local law enforcement in place for a takedown.* "We can meet back at the truck stop at one in the morning. That work for you?"

Butch shook his head. "Too much heat there right now. Wolverine will be in touch with the details. Tomorrow."

That was cutting far too close to the forty-eight-hour window his boss, Nash, had given him before pulling the plug on the investigation. "I told you my buyer's in a hurry."

"Tomorrow or no deal. I'm not a hundred percent believing everything you've told me. I need to make sure you're on the up-and-up. Wolverine will contact you at your shop, like always. That's the deal."

Ian didn't have to fake his frown. He wasn't happy with the delay, especially with Butch wanting to check his cover. It was solid, had stood up under heavy scrutiny so far. But no one had ever made the connection between Ian Savage and Ian McKenzie before either. Had he changed his appearance enough to fool anyone who might remember him from his high school days? He'd kept his visits to Gatlinburg centered around his family's cabin, never venturing into town as Ian McKenzie. Had he made a mistake somewhere? Was there anyone who knew his real identity aside from his family and Shannon?

He shrugged nonchalantly. "Just keep in mind that my buyer is a powerful, unforgiving man. If he expects a delivery, and you don't show, I wouldn't want to be in your shoes."

Butch narrowed his eyes. "And if you're actually Ian McKenzie, I wouldn't want to be in your shoes either." He clicked his thumb and forefinger at Ian as if he was pulling a trigger. Then he laughed and headed for the van.

Ian shot him the bird and then unlocked the door to the house. He went inside, slamming it behind him. Resisting the urge to flip the dead bolt, which the others would hear and assume he was worried about them, he left the door unlocked. He reached above one of the kitchen cabinets and took down the loaded shotgun he kept concealed there. Then he stood off to the side, aiming it at the door.

Seconds ticked by. A full minute. The van's engine started. A few seconds later, tires squealed as the van raced down the driveway. He yanked open the door, aiming his shotgun into the garage. Empty. No one was lying in wait. Butch and his thugs were gone.

He let out a deep breath before pressing the panel on the wall to close the garage door. This time, when he went inside the house, he flipped the dead bolt. He was reaching up to stow the shotgun when a shadow moved off to his right. He spun around.

"Whoa, whoa, it's me, Adam." A hand shoved his gun up toward the ceiling.

The lights flipped on. His brother stood a few feet away. Behind him, off to the side with her hand on the light switch, was Shannon.

Ian tucked the gun back above the cabinet. "What the hell, Adam? I could have killed you. And what are you doing here, Shannon?"

She stiffened. "We were saving you. Adam saw me in the parking lot at the hospital right after those guys abducted you. He drove me here so we could keep you from getting killed."

He speared his brother with a look of disgust. "You drove her here, knowing those guys were with me? You put her smack in the middle of danger."

"Kind of like you did at the truck stop?"

Ian took a menacing step toward his brother.

Adam raised his hands in surrender. "She was coming after you with or without me. I came along to keep her safe and help you. Instead of yelling at us, you should thank us. No telling what would have happened if she hadn't jumped in your car to rescue you. We scared those guys off."

Ian's eyes widened. "What do you mean you scared them off?" He looked toward the front windows. Red and blue lights flashed against the blinds. "You called the cops?"

Adam put his hands on his hips. "Well, of course I called the police. I figure those thugs saw the lights coming up the street and that's why they left. If I hadn't called the cops, those jerks would have stormed your house and filled you with bullet holes by now. What's your problem? Do you have to turn everything into a fight?"

"I'm trying to maintain my cover, no thanks to you. I had those guys ninety-nine percent convinced there's no connection between you and me, even though they recognized you as a cop. If they saw you come inside—"

"They didn't. We parked on a side street and came in through Shannon's half of the duplex, the door in the hall closet you two use for going back and forth."

The door Ian had put in when they'd begun their odd working relationship. A door they'd used more and more often, far too regularly to justify it as just because of their mutual desire to find Maria. The look on Adam's face said he suspected as much.

Ian didn't care what he thought. What he cared about was that Shannon had been placed in danger, and whether his whole case was now ruined. He'd been so close. Would this destroy the deal he'd just made? He would have said as much, but the disappointment on Shannon's face had him biting back his harsh words.

"Look, I appreciate that you were trying to help. Both of you. I honestly do. But I was negotiating with Butch, setting up a—"

A loud knock sounded on the front door. "Gatlinburg Police."

"Great." Ian shook his head. "The only way

I'm getting out of this with my cover intact is if they arrest me. For something." He gave his brother a baleful look. "I don't suppose you'd mind if I punch you when they bust down the door?"

Adam narrowed his eyes in warning.

"Yeah. Didn't think so."

"Police! Open up!" Loud knocks sounded on the door.

"Go on." Ian motioned toward the hall. "You two get back to the other side of the duplex. I'll think of something. And, Adam, don't go to the jail to bail me out. That would ruin everything. Can you just let my boss know what's going on? Please? He'll get me out without blowing my cover."

Adam gave him a curt nod, then urged Shannon to the hallway. They disappeared into the closet.

The police were kicking the front door now. It was a cheap door. No need for a battering ram. It wouldn't hold much longer. Ian turned, desperately looking for something that would get him locked up, hopefully without getting shot. Then he remembered the weed he'd taken from some punks a few days ago to keep them from selling it to neighborhood kids. He'd come into the garage and tossed it in a kitchen drawer, intending to get rid of it later and never had.

He yanked open a kitchen drawer, grabbed the baggie and tossed it onto the countertop in front of him just as the door crashed open and slammed against the wall.

"Freeze!" Two cops pointed their pistols at him.

He slowly raised his hands.

Chapter Nine

Shannon snapped the lid closed on her tattered suitcase. But instead of picking it up, she plopped down onto the bed beside it. The eggs and toast she'd eaten for breakfast sat like lead in her stomach. Worry and anger and despair were tearing her apart, physically and emotionally. Should she stay or should she go? The answer seemed to be eluding her.

She glanced around the room she'd slept in for the past six months. It wasn't much to look at, just big enough for the full-size bed. Her clothes were normally folded in cardboard boxes inside the closet. The rest of the rental was pretty much the same—a three-piece bathroom, galley-style kitchen with laminate counters, and a living room barely big enough for the worn love seat and a folding chair. The peeling fake-brass fixtures in the kitchen and the stained brown carpet had gone out of style decades ago. But the place still had more pluses than minuses.

Like the single-car garage with an automatic door opener that kept her from getting soaked in the rain or snow when she brought groceries home.

A charming foyer that boasted a surprisingly large coat closet.

A deep front porch with gleaming white railings and a swing. She sat out there most evenings, watching the neighborhood children play, wistfully wondering what it would have felt like to be so carefree when she was a little girl—instead of looking over her shoulder all the time, trying to stay out of the clutches of her mother's constant stream of "boyfriends."

In a word, the duplex was *home*. The first place that had ever felt that way. She'd started a life here, a real life, with a real job as a restaurant hostess at one of the resort hotels overlooking town. She'd even managed to tuck a little bit into savings. At twenty-one, she was finally her own person, making her own decisions, and looking forward to the future. Leaving this place would feel like she was going backward, starting over. Worst of all, it would mean not seeing Ian every day, maybe never seeing him again.

She dropped her head in her hands. It had taken months for him to work past her defenses. Months of gentle smiles, front porch hellos, the half-dozen times he'd insisted on fixing her pathetic car then refused to let her pay him. He'd earned her trust and had begun to wiggle his way into her heart.

After a few too many glasses of wine one evening, she'd confessed all the dirty secrets about her past. Instead of being disgusted, he'd been furious on her behalf. He held her through her tears, vowed to keep her safe and demanded nothing in return. *She* was the one who'd pushed for more, breaking down *his* defenses over time. Eventually, he too had confessed about the turmoil with his father, before his parents had been killed and he'd been put in foster care. It was his deepest secret.

Or so she'd thought.

It turned out he hadn't told her the most important secret of all—that he was a cop, and that his interest in helping her find her friend Maria was all about his job, not that he cared about Shannon and wanted to help her. Was anything they'd shared real?

Was what he'd told her about his father true or had he made that up too? If he'd grown up in foster care, how could his three brothers have been at the hospital today? None of it made sense. She didn't know what to believe. Or what to do. Because in spite of everything, she still cared about him.

"What's with the suitcase?"

She jerked her head up. Over six feet of mouthwatering male lounged in her doorway, looking so handsome it nearly shredded her heart. The cuts and bruises only made him look tougher, cooler. She hated the relief that flooded through her, the yearning that had her curling her fingers against the mattress to keep from jumping up and throwing herself into his arms. Ever since the police had hauled him away, she'd been terrified that she'd never see him again.

And equally terrified that she might.

"How did you get out of jail so fast?" Score one point for her. She'd managed to speak without bursting into tears.

His mouth curled in one of those sexy half smiles of his. "The old-fashioned way. I made bail."

She glanced at the clock on the wall. "A judge set bail at eight o'clock in the morning?"

"I might have had my boss pull a few strings behind the scenes." His smile faded. "You okay? My brother didn't harass you, did he?"

She shook her head. "No. He was…nice.

For a cop." She waved toward the sling on his left arm. "And for a guy who beat the crap out of his own brother."

He straightened and took two steps forward, which placed him squarely at the foot of her bed, forcing her to look up to meet his blue-eyed gaze. She used to think no one could possibly have eyes that particular gorgeous shade of blue, like a mountain lake after a summer shower. Until she'd met his brothers. She clutched the bedspread harder, this time to keep from slugging him for all the lies he'd told her.

"All my brothers and I have beaten the crap out of each other over the years. It's pretty normal, or so I hear. Too much testosterone, I guess. There's a lot more fighting than hugging in my family. But we don't mean anything by it. Usually."

She shook her head. "You have three brothers. And every one of them is a cop. What are the odds of that?"

"It's a family tradition. My dad's a retired federal judge. And very much alive, in spite of what I told you."

She stared at him in shock, more freaked out over his father's occupation than to learn that he wasn't really dead. "He's alive? And he was a federal judge?"

"He is. He was." He drew a deep breath, let it out. "My father was a force to be reckoned with, back in the day, for more reasons than you and I ever spoke about. Everyone looked up to him, happy to do his bidding. He had tentacles in every alphabet agency and attorney's office this side of the Mississippi. Governors, state legislators, attorneys on both sides of the aisle came to him for advice. They probably still do. They don't call him Mighty McKenzie for nothing."

She blinked. "Mighty McKenzie? Good grief. What did your mom think of all of that? Oh, wait. She's probably still alive too, right? The orphan, Ian Savage, seems to be overflowing in the family department these days."

He gave her a solemn look. "I thank God that, yes, my mom is still alive and doing well. I visit her once or twice a year. It's all I can stomach because it means seeing my dad too, and sometimes my brothers. She's a retired prosecutor."

"Well, of course she is." She rolled her eyes. "Is the family dog a K9 police officer too?"

He crouched in front of her, close, but not touching. The look of yearning and regret in his eyes nearly stole her breath. "I'm so sorry, Shannon. I never meant to hurt you."

She swallowed against the tightness in her throat. "But you did. Hurt me."

"I know."

"You lied to me. Not little lies either. Doozies."

His mouth quirked. "Doozies?"

"Don't make fun of me. I'm not in the mood."

He sobered. "Sorry. Again. Yes, I lied. Great big lies. Doozies."

He reached out as if to brush aside her bangs, but she jerked back before he could touch her. He sighed and dropped his hand.

"I never told you that I was with Homeland Security, that I was working undercover. I fed you the same backstory I'd told others, so I could maintain my cover. But everything else, what really matters, was true." His gaze searched hers. *"Everything."*

The kissing, the make-out sessions on her couch.

"What you told me about your father, about Willow, was that a lie too?"

He winced. "No. That was true, every word. I've never talked to anyone about that time in my life. Except you."

He was being charming, and sweet, and making her want to believe him so badly that she ached. *Don't be a fool.* She couldn't allow herself to fall for his lies, not again.

"You said your father died. That you never knew your mother, that you were an only child."

"I did. That was part of my—"

"Cover. So that you could catch the bad guys."

He nodded, his still-sad eyes watching her intently. Did he think she could just work this out of her system? That he'd answer a few questions and they could go back to being… whatever they were?

"There's something that has me stumped," she said. "I can't figure out what you got out of pretending to be my friend, pretending to care."

He blew out a deep breath before straightening. He leaned back against the wall, his gaze never leaving hers. "I wasn't pretending. I am your friend. I do care."

She shook her head. "No. You aren't. You don't. I told you about my past, and you pretended that it mattered to you. You said you wanted to go after those traffickers, at the truck stop, so you could keep other girls from suffering what I went through. That was cruel, Ian. How could you use my pain like that? You had to be laughing inside the whole time at how gullible I was."

He was shaking his head before she finished. "I've *never* laughed at you, Shannon.

You're a strong, independent woman. Most of all, you're a survivor. I admire you."

She stiffened. "Don't. Don't stand there trying to charm me and tell more lies—"

"No lies. No hidden agendas. Ask me anything. I promise you I'll tell the truth."

She blinked. "Anything? You'll answer any question?"

He nodded. "I owe you that."

She thought a moment, then asked, "Why did you befriend me?"

His eyes widened with surprise. "Have you looked in the mirror lately?"

She glanced at the cracked oval mirror hanging on the wall beside the door, thinking about what she saw every time she looked at her reflection. "I see an average-looking woman with hair that refuses to lie the way I want it to. I'm short, too skinny, flat-chested with almost no butt. I'm the exact opposite of what guys like you look for in a woman."

His dark brows arched. "Guys like me?"

She refused to flatter his ego by stating the obvious—that he was the definition of gorgeous. Tall, buff, with a smile that could melt butter. It had definitely melted her on more than one occasion. She crossed her arms and waited.

"Okay, truth. You're the perfect height for

me to tuck you against my side. You're slim, not skinny. Most girls would kill for your flat tummy and those curvy hips. Your... ah, chest is perfectly proportioned for your frame. And the rest of you, well, in case you haven't noticed, you've revved my engine plenty of times. There's absolutely nothing lacking about you in the looks department. Guys like me—whatever that means—would line up just to get a woman like you to smile at them. Top that off with your brains and a great sense of humor, and you're basically irresistible."

All the warm squishy feelings flooding through her at his words died a quick death with his last statement. She crossed her arms. "Irresistible? Right. That's why you always came up with an excuse whenever we got hot and heavy. Instead of taking things to the logical next level—" she motioned toward the bed "—you always came up with a reason to leave. That's not what I'd call irresistible."

He pushed away from the wall and knelt in front of her again. Before she realized what he was going to do, he'd taken her hand in his. With his intent gaze locked on hers, he slowly drew her hand to his chest, then slid it down, down, down. She sucked in a breath when it dawned on her what he was doing, and that he was giving her the opportunity to stop him if she wanted to.

She couldn't have stopped him any more than she could have given up air.

With his hand on hers, he cupped himself through his jeans. The hard length of him warmed her fingers. She let out a shuddering breath.

"That's what you do to me, Shannon. Just thinking about touching you, kissing you, loving you, I get a hard-on. That's not something I can fake or lie about."

Her pulse was rushing in her ears. All this time, she'd craved touching him this way. But it wasn't right; nothing was right anymore. She drew a ragged breath and forced herself to tug her hand away.

He dropped his hand to his side. "It would have been wrong to make love to you while my fake identity stood between us. It was torture keeping my hands off you." He searched her gaze, then let out a deep sigh and stood again. "You can't forgive me, can you?"

"You never asked."

He hesitated, studying her. "Will you forgive me?"

Yes. No. She wanted to, so badly. But would she be letting him back in her heart to hurt her yet again? She drew another ragged breath, then shook her head. "I can't. Not yet."

"Not ever?"

"Maybe. I honestly don't know."

His jaw tightened. "I understand. It's probably for the best, anyway. Once this case is over, I'll go on to another one, in another town, maybe another state." He shrugged. "You've made a good life here. And one day you'll meet the perfect guy for you, one who's willing to give up his career and settle down. You deserve that. You deserve to be treated like a queen. You deserve to be happy." He stepped forward and pressed a kiss against her forehead, then moved to the doorway.

His words were still tightening like a band around her chest when he looked back. "I never got a chance to tell you last night. But Butch showed me more pictures in the garage. One of them was Maria."

She pressed a hand to her throat. "Are you sure?"

"As sure as I can be. Same build and general features you described. And a pink butterfly on the right side of her neck. Wolverine's supposed to contact me at the shop sometime today to agree on where to make the exchange. If everything goes as planned, your friend will be freed by this evening."

He started to leave, but she jumped up and grabbed his good arm, stopping him. "Wait. Your arm was nearly broken, your *gun* arm. And you've got a concussion. Doesn't Homeland Security have someone else who can take care of this?"

He shook his head. "It took me months to gain Wolverine's and Butch's trust. That trust is hanging by a thread. If I leave and someone new tries to get in on the action, that thread will snap. Butch and his guys will take their victims somewhere else, and I'll lose my chance to help those girls. Your friend Maria will disappear again. No telling how long it would take to find her, or if she'll even still be alive the next time we get a lead on her whereabouts. You know how violent and unpredictable the sex trade can be. I have to do this, try to rescue all of them, including Maria."

"No."

He frowned. "No? You don't want me to rescue your friend?"

"Of course I do. But it's too dangerous for you to do it alone. If Homeland Security won't help you, then I will." She held up her hands. "I still have the use of both my arms. And I didn't escape the sex trade through brains and tenacity alone. I can fire a gun as well as or better than you."

His eyes narrowed. "You've never mentioned that before."

She lifted her chin. "It didn't seem relevant."

He rubbed his hand on the back of his neck. "I wish we had more time to discuss this. But I have to get going or risk missing Wolverine's call at the shop. Don't worry about me, Shannon. I may be the only agent in plain sight, but I've got backup ready to go the moment I need them. I'm not in this alone. I'll be okay. And there's no way that I'm going to take you with me into danger again. Yesterday could have ended in disaster for you. I don't need, or want, your help." He left her sputtering as he disappeared down the hallway.

She ran after him. "Ian."

He ignored her as he opened the hall closet door where the panel between the two sides of the duplex was hidden. He slid it open and she grabbed his arm.

"Ian, wait."

He looked back at her, his expression hard. "You could have been killed yesterday, Shannon. Butch and his men know where I live. They could be watching this place even now. You should lie low. Stay inside. Don't go out on the porch. Keep the shades drawn. Until this is over, you stay on your side and I'll stay on mine. I don't want to see you anywhere near the shop. No arguments."

He stepped through the panel and slid it shut.

She stood there fuming for several moments. Then she shoved the panel, determined to finish their discussion. The panel didn't budge. She frowned and pressed it again. Then she remembered the locking mechanisms on both sides. Neither of them had ever locked each other out. Until now.

Chapter Ten

Ian slid his ID badge through the card reader hanging on the shop's wall to clock in.

"Seven o'clock was two hours ago, Savage."

He turned around to see Ralph Sanders, owner of Sanders Auto Repair, standing beside the 1969 red Mustang whose carburetor Ian was supposed to rebuild this morning.

"Sorry, boss. Had a little trouble last night."

His boss motioned toward Ian's face. "What's the other guy look like?"

"Unfortunately, a lot better than me." He'd left his sling in his Charger and downed several pain pills, determined to force his way through the pain since he'd need both hands to work on cars today. But there was nothing he could do to hide the cuts and bruises on his face. He nodded toward the Mustang. "I'll get right on that. Shouldn't take long to get it running like new."

"The owner's leaving town this morning. I

didn't know if you'd show up or not, so I had Andy work on it."

Ian groaned. "You didn't."

"There wasn't anyone else available. I didn't have a choice." He checked the old-fashioned gold-toned watch on his wrist. "You've got forty-three minutes to figure out what our beginner mechanic screwed up and get that car purring like a kitten."

"Where's the kid now?"

"After he put the fire out, I assigned him to delivery duty for the day. He's on his way to pick up a set of tires for a customer."

"Fire?" Dread shot through him as he glanced at the classic sports car that would have been the envy of every boy with a pulse back in high school. Its current owner kept it in pristine condition, coddling it like a baby. "I don't see any burn marks. What's the damage?"

"Pop the hood. You'll see." He checked his watch. "Forty-two minutes and counting. Don't let me down, Savage. The owner's fanaticism about bringing that car in for the slightest little hiccup pays my light bill every month. I can't afford to lose his business." He strode toward the other side of the garage where another mechanic was replacing brake pads beneath a truck on a hydraulic lift.

When Ian raised the Mustang's hood, he immediately knew why his boss had sent his novice apprentice out on deliveries. If the kid had been standing here right now, Ian would have blistered his pride with a lecture that would have had his ears ringing the rest of the day. Not because of the damage to the car—a melted distributor cap and wires. Those were easily fixed. Ian wasn't even angry that the kid had installed the carburetor float upside down, which must have been what had caused gas to shoot up and coat the distributor cap. What had him fuming was the source of the spark that had started the fire—a charred half-smoked cigarette butt lying on top of the battery. The foolish kid was lucky he hadn't killed himself, or at the least ended up with debilitating burns. Ian's brother Colin had spent months in a burn center after saving some people from a burning building and was left with deep scars on his arms and chest. Ian wouldn't want anyone to suffer the way his brother had. He shook his head in disgust and got to work.

By the time the Mustang's owner arrived, the engine was purring like a kitten and all evidence of the fire had been removed. Sanders nodded his approval from across the bay. But it was clear as the day wore on that Ian still wasn't forgiven for being late and, in Sanders's mind, almost losing him a treasured repeat client. Every mind-numbingly dull and dirty job that came in was routed to Ian. He was so busy he could barely catch his breath, although he did stop several times to take more pain pills. It was that or admit defeat.

His left arm was throbbing when he noticed the sun was sinking on the horizon outside the open bay doors. It was quitting time. But he still hadn't heard from Wolverine. After washing the grime off his hands and clocking out, he knew why. Wolverine didn't *need* to call in order to reach Ian. He was already here, lounging in his bright yellow VW across the street in Sanders's overflow gravel lot.

Fast-food bags tossed onto the ground outside the car told the story. He'd been performing surveillance on Ian all day, and Ian had been too consumed pushing through the pain of his wrenched arm to even realize it. Having Butch's thug spying on him wasn't half as alarming as the fact that he hadn't noticed. That kind of mistake could get him killed.

He nodded goodbye to some of the guys from the shop, promised his boss he'd call the next time he was running late, then headed across the street. He idled his Charger beside the VW and rolled down his driver's-side window.

"What's with the cloak-and-dagger spy routine, Wolverine? If you wanted to talk to me, all you have to do is step into the shop."

Wolverine grinned. "Cloak-and-dagger. I like that."

Ian arched a brow, his patience nonexistent after the pain-filled, aggravating day he'd had. What a waste. He had precious little time remaining to bring this case to a close or all of his months of undercover would be for nothing. "I'm tired and hungry and have to give my buyer an update. Do we have a deal or not?"

"Whoa. Chill, bro." He cocked his head as if studying Ian. "You seem really stressed out, man. When's the last time you and that hot chick next door hooked up?"

Cold fear shot through Ian. Had Butch seen Shannon? Did he recognize her from the truck stop and think she was a threat, that maybe she knew too much? He kept his expression bland and rolled his eyes.

"If you're talking about my duplex neighbor, the answer is never. I'm not her type."

Wolverine's brows shot up. "A handsome dude like you? You expect me to believe that?"

Ian gave him a droll look. "I don't have the

right kind of plumbing for her, if you get my meaning."

Wolverine grinned again. "She likes chicks, huh? Dang. That makes *me* hot."

"I have better things to do than discuss your fetishes. And I'm not wasting another minute on you or your boss. We're done here." He shifted into Drive.

"Hold it, hold it." He held his hands up in a placating gesture. "Man, you really are uptight tonight, aren't you?"

"Wolverine—"

"Okay. All right. Butch told me if no red flags were raised today, and he didn't call with anything from his side, that the deal is on. Eleven o'clock at a warehouse outside of town." He gave Ian the address. "Bring a truck and the money. You get there one minute late, no deal. There will be guns trained on you the moment you enter the parking lot. Bring someone with you, try anything at all, you're a dead man. Understood?"

Wolverine's transition from his usual jovial, silly personality to a threatening, deadly serious persona had the hairs rising on the back of Ian's neck, and alarm bells going off in his head.

Suddenly Wolverine grinned. "Did I do that good? Butch told me to try to keep it serious for once." He laughed and popped a french fry into his mouth, then grimaced and spit it out. "Old and cold. Well, what's it gonna be? Deal or no deal?"

"I'll be there."

"Cool, dude. You see? All those months ago, I told you I'd get you an in. I came through, didn't I?"

Ian smiled. "You sure did."

"And we'll make more deals with other buyers, right? That's what you said you wanted when we started, an *in* so we could both make some cash." He held out his hand and made the universal sign of money by rubbing his fingers together.

"No kickback until I have the girls."

Wolverine shrugged. "That's fine. But you better slip me my finder's fee without alerting Butch tonight. He realizes I'm getting money from both sides, I'm toast." He gave a dramatic shiver, then laughed and drove away.

Ian's smile faded as he watched the taillights of the garish yellow car fade into the distance, then turn down a side street. Something was off about his neighborhood human trafficking connection. Did Wolverine know something about tonight that Ian didn't? Was it a setup or was Butch really going to go through with the buy? Either way, Ian needed to be prepared. That meant getting a truck and backup, and making sure his fellow agents knew about the conditions that Butch had dictated, and the accompanying threats. They'd have to be very careful and precise, or someone might get killed.

He grabbed a pen and paper from his console and scribbled down some notes while he made the call to set everything in motion. "Tony's Pizza? I'd like to order a large pizza for curbside pickup. It's not on the menu, but one of the take-out guys—Chris—knows about it. I've gotten it there before. It's called the Homeland Special."

A few minutes later, Ian pulled into one of the curbside pickup spots on the side of the familiar redbrick building that boasted a neon sign on the roof in the shape of a slice of pizza.

It didn't take long for the take-out door to open and a young man in black jeans and a red T-shirt with the restaurant's logo on the front to come bopping out with a pizza box in his hands.

Ian rolled down his window. "Hey, Chris. How's business tonight?"

The young man's gaze locked on Ian with a seriousness that contrasted sharply with the polite smile he flashed. To anyone else in the parking lot, or watching from inside, he was simply a pizza boy. But Ian knew better.

"Hopping like always, Mr. Savage. Typical Friday night, barely enough time to catch my breath." He held up the box in his hands. "One large Homeland Special to go. Pepperoni, bacon, extra cheese, extra sauce, New York–style crust, well-done. That'll be—" he tilted the box to read the bottom of the ticket taped to the lid "—twenty-two fifty-seven."

Ian set the box on the seat beside him, then pulled out his wallet. He concealed a folded piece of paper inside a wad of bills and handed it out the window. "Keep the change."

Chris grinned and shoved the money along with the piece of paper into his pocket. "Thanks, Mr. Savage. Always a pleasure. Enjoy." With that, he hurried back inside.

Ian pulled out of the parking lot and headed for the duplex.

Chapter Eleven

A thumping sound had Shannon looking up from the Lisa Gardner thriller she was reading. The noise sounded again, and she realized it was coming from the hall closet. Ian. In a fit of anger, she'd locked her side of the panel too. And now he wanted to come in.

Someone with far more poise than her, someone more sophisticated, would have ignored his knock. Or at least made him wait, maybe even grovel a little bit. But Shannon was too pathetically relieved that he wanted to see her again that she ran to the closet and unlocked her side.

He slid open the door and they stood in the semidarkness looking at each other, with only the lights from their respective living rooms shining inside.

"Hey," he breathed.

She smiled. "Hey yourself." She moved

closer, then jumped back when she hit something sharp.

He grinned and held up a pizza box. "Sorry. I think you ran into the corner. You okay?"

She rubbed her chest. "Slain by cardboard. I think I'll live. Is that a peace offering?"

"Pepperoni, bacon, extra sauce, extra cheese."

"You're not playing fair. That's my favorite."

His grin widened. "I know." He held it toward her, his smile fading. "I didn't exactly leave on the best of terms earlier. I was a jerk, and I'm sorry. You're welcome to take this and enjoy it by yourself. I wouldn't blame you if you do."

"I'm not that petty. There's enough to share. Come on."

He followed her inside as she took the box to the bar that separated the kitchen from the living room. She used to have only one bar stool. But after he'd moved in next door, she'd hoped the gorgeous man would come over sometime, so she'd gotten another one. It was one of the best buying decisions she'd ever made. They'd shared many a pizza on this bar top while sitting on these bar stools.

She tossed some paper plates and napkins beside the box. "I see you aren't wearing your sling. Your arm can't be all better this fast."

"I can't do my job with the sling on. I'm taking pain pills when I need to." When she started to protest, he interrupted her. "I'm okay, Shannon. Honestly. But thanks for the concern."

She sighed and opened the refrigerator. "Want a beer? Wine?"

He shook his head. "Water's fine."

She hesitated. While Ian was never a heavy drinker, he rarely said no to a beer to go with his pizza. "Something going on tonight?" She handed him a water bottle and took the stool beside him.

As he set a piece on her plate, he arched a brow in question. "What do you mean?"

"No alcohol. Are you…are you still on the clock? As in doing special-agent kind of stuff?" Her eyes widened. "Is it Maria and the others? You finally made a deal?"

She waited impatiently for him to chew and swallow the bite of pizza he'd taken.

"A deal is in the works," he admitted, sounding reluctant. "But I'm not going to discuss it. You know far too much about me as it is. It's not safe for you to know more."

"I'm not trying to get in the way or put myself in danger. But if you're going to rescue Maria and the others soon, I'd like to be there, to help with their transition."

"There will be counselors for them as soon as we get them out of danger."

She shook her head. "Take it from some-one who knows. It would take months, maybe longer, for someone coming out of that life to learn to trust someone enough to talk about it. In the meantime, they'll be scared, con-fused. Having someone who's been through what they've been through could really help. Use me. Seriously. I want to do this. Can't I wait somewhere close by? Then as soon as you have the bad guys in cuffs, let me come out? I haven't seen Maria in so long. I need to see her, talk to her, tell her—"

He stood and tossed his half-eaten piece onto his plate. "Coming over was a mistake. As soon as I have something concrete on your friend, I'll let you know."

Regret had her chasing after him and jump-ing in front of the closet door. "Ian. Wait. I'm sorry. I don't want to fight again."

He braced his good arm on the door frame. "I can't discuss the case or any plans I'm making."

"I know. I understand, really. I'm disap-pointed, but I get it." She gave him a friendly tap on the chest. "Come on. I was so upset this morning I called out at work. This is ba-sically the first day I've had off in two weeks. Let's not ruin it by being angry with each other." She held out her hand toward his. "Eat some more pizza with me. Maybe watch a movie on TV. We'll pretend we're two normal people without any baggage or secret-agent jobs between us and just enjoy each other. Okay?"

He smiled and then kissed her on the forehead before taking her hand. "All right. Dinner and a movie. No work talk."

They both stuck to their agreement, and before long they were laughing and talking and then tucked in close beside each other on the couch with a blanket over the both of them as they watched one of her favorite movies—*Sabrina*. It was the original, the black-and-white one with Audrey Hepburn. It never failed to make her cry, both sad tears and happy ones when the girl got her guy at the end.

With all those feelings swirling around inside, when she looked up at the gorgeous man smiling at her, she couldn't resist pulling him down for a kiss. He accommodated her nicely, his lips moving expertly over hers, quickening her pulse and making her jealous at the same time. How many women did a guy have to kiss in his life to get this good at it? She immediately wanted to rip out their hair and thank them at the same time.

He pulled back and framed her face in his hands. "You really are beautiful, Shannon Murphy."

Her body went all soft and warm at his words. "So are you, Ian Savage." She blinked, some of the delicious feelings fading beneath the onslaught of reality. "I mean McKenzie. Special Agent McKenzie." She pushed out of his arms, suddenly feeling awkward with the man who'd been her best friend until yesterday.

"Is that really such a bad thing?" His voice sounded sad.

She shrugged. "It's going to take some getting used to. I'm still processing the fact that I'm sleeping with the enemy." Her face heated. "So to speak. I mean, it's not like we've ever…you know." She frowned. "Why is that again?"

His brows drew down. "Imagine if we had, and then you found out who I really am. You would have felt—"

"Violated."

He winced, then nodded. "Is that how you feel now?"

She wrapped her arms around her middle, unable to meet his gaze. "Don't be silly. Of course not. You're not like the cops in my old life, the ones on the take, who traded sex with my mom and others in exchange for not arresting them." She shivered at the memories. "Or ignored a little girl asking for help, telling them her mom's boyfriends were hurting her."

He gently tilted her chin up. "I'm so sorry that happened to you. But being a cop is like any other profession. There are good people and bad people. Thankfully, the training and oversight weed out most of the bad. I'm far from perfect, but I like to think I'm one of the good ones."

She knew he was right, that he was one of the good ones, even if she didn't believe that the rest of them were more good than bad. But just the reminder about who he was and that he'd fooled her for so long had anger simmering inside her again. "Maybe you should head back home now. It's getting late."

He glanced at the sleek black watch on his right wrist, an anachronism since most men as young as him didn't wear a watch. She'd always wondered at that before. Now she realized it was probably because of his job. No doubt he needed to be aware of the time at a moment's notice, quicker than it took to take out his phone and check it, so he could coordinate missions with his fellow agents.

"It's later than I realized." He stood. "Thanks for sharing dinner and a movie with me. We'll talk more tomorrow. Okay?"

She nodded, but she didn't get up when he headed down the hall to the pass-through. Instead, she sat there a long time thinking about what she knew and didn't know about Ian McKenzie. Actually, all she knew about him as *McKenzie* was that he worked for Homeland Security. And that he had a family—a mom, dad and three brothers. That was pretty much it. Everything she knew, or thought she knew, was about Ian *Savage*.

Did she really know Ian at all?

As she put her treasured DVD of *Sabrina* away and straightened up the kitchen, memories of times she'd spent with him flashed through her mind. He'd always been patient, kind, protective. He'd shared his smiles and always made a point of bringing her favorite pizza when he brought her dinner. She'd really been falling for *that* Ian. The problem was that she didn't know which Ian was the real one.

As always when she was upset or mulling over a problem, she started cleaning. But her house was fairly clean to begin with. It was so tiny she had to keep it picked up or she'd kill herself tripping over things. It didn't take long before it was sparkling. Of course, that meant she was back to thinking about Ian again. And Maria. And how long it would be before Maria was free. And on and on and on. She finally realized she'd never be able to relax or sleep tonight. Too much had happened in the past few days. She needed that promised talk with Ian right now, not later.

She went to the hall closet to check if he was still home and slid the panel open. She'd stepped into his side of the closet and was about to open the door when she heard a man's voice.

And it wasn't Ian's.

She pressed her ear to the cheap hollow door that did little to dampen sound, then breathed a sigh of relief when she heard Ian's deep voice in answer to whatever the man had asked. When Ian responded, he called the man Chris. She'd never heard him mention anyone named Chris before. That wasn't the name of one of the mechanics from the shop. In fact, this was the first time that she'd known him to have anyone else in the duplex, besides her. But their voices weren't raised in anger, so the man must be a friend—not one of Butch's thugs or even one of Ian's brothers.

She was about to return to her place when she heard Ian mention *her* name. Unabashedly curious as to why he'd talk about her with someone she'd never met, she pressed her ear to the door again.

"—Wolverine seemed way too interested in her when we spoke earlier today," Ian said. "That's why I came straight here after passing you that note at the pizza place. I needed to see for myself that Shannon was okay, that no one had bothered her."

Shannon's heart sank. Had he come by only to check on her well-being? He'd gone there because he felt obligated, because it was his job to make sure no one was hurt while he was trying to wheel and deal with the dregs of society.

"Does he think she knows something? Or that she and you are an item and he wants to use her as leverage?"

"I don't see how. We're casual friends because we rent two sides of the same house. That's it. I guarantee that even if Wolverine has been watching this place, the most he would have seen is us talking on occasion or me working on her car."

His casual-friends comment had her heart twisting in her chest.

"But you still want me to keep an eye on the place?" the other man asked.

"Just for tonight, until the deal is done. I can't risk any civilians getting hurt. Once Butch and the others are in custody and we've rescued the victims, any potential for danger will be over. Okay, Chris, now it's your turn. Tell me what Nash has planned. We have to make sure no one is seen anywhere near the warehouse. Wolverine said Butch's men would kill anyone out there, that I'm to go alone."

"Nash brought ADA Ellison up to speed, and he's going to provide logistical support and—"

She blinked in shock as Ian and Chris discussed the details of the transaction, planned for this very night in just a few hours, at a warehouse outside of town. She recognized the location. It had been a trail-horse stable at one time, but the recent wildfires in the area had destroyed all of the fencing and the house. While the horses had been spared, the owner didn't have insurance. He'd had to sell them and the land.

It had been sad seeing a row of warehouses go up where the stable had once been. Even more shocking was that the warehouses were being used by Butch and his men. Was that where Maria and the others were being housed in between being forced to turn tricks or perform in porn movies that would be distributed across the dark web?

Ian's deep voice broke into her thoughts. "I've shown you where everything is. Any other questions?"

"Just one. Where do you keep the beer?"

Ian laughed. "None of that, Chris. Sober is your middle name while you're on guard duty.

But I do have a couple of steaks you can pop in the broiler if you get hungry."

The sound of their footsteps retreating across the room into the kitchen had her tripping over her own feet in a hurry to get back to her side of the duplex. She slid down onto the couch and dropped her face into her hands. How could Ian have kissed her so sweetly earlier, and several other times, and then act like they were barely even friends? His voice had been so matter-of-fact, so… businesslike when he'd talked about her. Was she really just that, a job, a civilian to protect while he was forced to live here for his undercover work? What would happen when the case was over and he moved on to the next case? Would he just disappear one day? Would he even bother to say goodbye?

Good grief, how had she fallen so hard and so fast for him? She was acting like some lovestruck teenager instead of a grown woman who'd survived some of the worst abuse imaginable. She'd survived, escaped and begun a new life. She was stronger than this. So why did it hurt so much?

She sat there a long time, furiously trying to get back her equilibrium and her confidence. The metallic screech of Ian's garage door opening had her lifting her head. A moment later the throaty roar of his Charger started up. It slowly faded into the distance. He was off to the warehouse, to finally get Maria and the others. He didn't want her help. He didn't even want her, period. But she wasn't going to sit here feeling sorry for herself any longer.

Maria was what mattered.

All those young women were what mattered. She'd been in their place before, sold into modern-day slavery by her very own mother. And it had taken years to find her way back to freedom. It had been Maria who'd covered for her so Shannon could finally escape. When the hunt had died down, and Shannon was able to sneak back to try to help Maria get out too—she was gone, sold to yet another buyer.

Now, with Maria found once again and about to be freed, Shannon wasn't about to miss that moment and not be there for her friend. No matter what Ian wanted. Shannon wouldn't interfere. But she was determined to be ready once it was over, and help the woman who'd once helped her.

Still, she knew all about the dangers of this kind of world, the kind where slavery still existed and destroyed lives. A world with large amounts of money at stake. The men and women who ran it were rabid about defending their livelihood. Shannon needed to be prepared in case things went horribly wrong.

She headed into her bedroom and went to the far back corner. After sliding the TV tray that she used as a nightstand out of the way, she pried up a scuffed piece of the wood flooring to reveal a dark hole. Reaching inside, she drew out her savings, a roll of bills held together by a ponytail holder. She peeled off two bills and dropped them back into the hole as her emergency fund. The rest she shoved into her jeans pocket. Finally she'd be able to pay Maria back for the money she'd given Shannon all those years ago. It was money Maria was supposed to give her "owner" later that night, the haul from that day's tricks. And she'd likely paid the balance in flesh when she'd had nothing to turn over at the end of the evening. Now it was Shannon's turn to pay her back as best she could.

But that wasn't all that she kept in her little cubbyhole. Money wasn't the only thing her friend had given her so very long ago.

She reached down again and pulled out a pistol.

Chapter Twelve

Ian itched to get out of the eighteen-foot rental truck and go into the warehouse. But his boss was adamant that he wait in the parking lot for Butch and the others to show. Because of Ian's history with Butch taking him at gunpoint, and Butch's earlier suspicion that Ian's cover might not be real, Nash wasn't taking any chances. Which had Ian frustrated as hell. He didn't join Homeland Security to sit in the cab of a truck waiting for the bad guy to show. And waiting was all he'd been doing for the past hour.

He checked his watch yet again. Almost midnight. He scanned the empty parking lot and surrounding tree line for the hundredth time. Nothing. Not even headlights flashing in the distance, indicating a vehicle was coming up the mountain. He'd followed Wolverine's instructions, had gotten here a few minutes before eleven, mindful of the warning that if he was late the deal was off. He hadn't been late. His knocks on the door of the warehouse had gone unanswered before he'd returned to the truck to wait. So why hadn't Butch and his men shown up?

The radio in the truck squawked. "Heard anything from them?" Nash asked.

Determined not to risk even moving his lips in case Butch was out there watching, he tapped twice on the transmitter, indicating no.

"Ellison is pushing us to raid the warehouse. He claims probable cause, wants to go in."

Ian tightened his grip on the steering wheel. If this was a test to find out if Ian was a cop, if Butch was watching to make sure that Ian was alone, then raiding the warehouse now would ruin everything. He tapped twice on the transmitter again, hard.

A sigh sounded from his boss. "I don't know that I can put him off much longer. He's insistent. And he's got plenty of officers with him. He doesn't have to wait for us. If those women are inside the warehouse, or if your contact got scared and took off, I want Homeland Security to be the first on scene to get the credit. I think we should move in soon. Something has either spooked your guy or—"

Ian shoved the door open and hopped out

of the truck, ignoring his boss's alarmed calls through the radio. He slammed the door shut and stalked toward the warehouse. If his contacts were here, maybe going inside would be the push they needed. If it had been up to him, he'd have gone inside long ago. And if Gatlinburg PD and his fellow agents were about to pour down the mountainside into the parking lot, this was his last chance to get in ahead of them and hopefully salvage the deal.

He crossed his fingers that his gut was wrong, that he hadn't been sitting in that truck for over an hour for nothing. That all of his months of hard work hadn't been thrown away because one of his brothers happened by the same truck stop as him. If the warehouse was empty, then Butch had decided not to make the deal. Which meant something had spooked him and he was likely on his way out of town already with his haul.

And Ian wouldn't be able to save Maria or the others.

He reached the door to the warehouse and cautiously turned the handle. It wasn't locked, yet another bad sign. If there was something inside worth protecting, the door would have been padlocked from the outside, maybe even barred from within with a guard inside.

He yanked out his pistol, then pulled open

the door and ran inside, sweeping his gun back and forth. The lights had turned on automatically. They must have been on a motion sensor. And what they revealed made him sick to his stomach. The warehouse was empty.

Ian prayed his boss kept everyone outside until he had a chance to find out what was going on. They'd all concealed their vehicles at the bottom of the mountain and had hiked through the woods, in the cold, to get here. They'd been hiding for hours, well before the planned meeting time to ensure that Butch didn't see them. Hopefully all of that work wouldn't be thrown away because of some impatient ADA pushing everyone to run into the warehouse before Ian had a chance to see if there was anything left to salvage.

Even though the place seemed empty, there were some doors on the back and sides, going into other rooms. He made a complete circuit of the interior, keeping his gun out as he checked every potential hiding place. But every door he opened revealed the same thing—nothing—until he reached the very last door. He yanked it open, sweeping his pistol back and forth. There was no one there, not even a piece of furniture, like the other rooms he'd tried. But there was something, a bright yellow index card dead center in the middle of the floor.

He rushed forward and crouched to read the card. He scanned it, then jerked his head up toward the ceiling. The sounds of shouting and doors being thrown open had him grabbing his pistol and aiming it at the door.

It burst open and his boss stood in the opening, flanked by half a dozen agents in full body armor, pistols drawn.

"Hold your fire! He's one of us," Nash yelled, as the agents swarmed in beside him.

Ian swore and shoved his gun into his holster. The other agents rushed back out of the room, presumably to search the rest of the warehouse.

Ian swore again, shaking his head. "You couldn't give me even five minutes in here before bringing in the damn cavalry?"

Nash frowned as he holstered his gun. "You were supposed to wait in the truck, and you went in without backup. What did you expect me to do?" He thumped Ian's chest. "And you were supposed to wear your vest, McKenzie."

Ian pointed up at the ceiling and repeated the words written on the index card. "Smile for the camera."

Nash looked up, his face going pale as he

noticed the red blinking light. He looked at Ian. "What's going on?"

Ian motioned toward the index card. "Butch was testing me, to make sure I'd follow orders and wouldn't bring anyone from law enforcement. The card has instructions to meet Wolverine tomorrow in the parking lot across from the garage where I work. He'll give me the true meeting time and place, but only if I passed tonight's test. And then it said to look up and smile for the camera." Ian shook his head. "It was a freaking test. And we just failed the hell out of it. No way will Wolverine meet me tomorrow. Six months wasted. All those girls, those little girls—" He fisted his hands and stalked out of the room.

He left the collection of the index card to his boss. Not that it would matter. It wasn't like any fingerprints or trace evidence would have been left on it to help them find Butch and his victims. He was too smart for that.

Ian wove his way through the cops and agents milling around the parking lot and was halfway to the truck when he noticed familiar dark hair with blue tips as a woman was led toward him by a Gatlinburg police officer.

Shannon. Her hands were cuffed behind her. By the time he'd reached her and the officer who'd detained her, Nash and Assistant District Attorney Ellison had caught up to him.

"Let her go," Ian snarled. "She's a civilian and not associated with the traffickers."

The officer shook his head. "I've placed her under arrest. She was hiding in the bushes at the edge of the lot and was armed." He pointed to a pistol shoved into his utility belt.

Ian stared at Shannon in disbelief.

She stared defiantly back at him. "I wanted to be here for Maria, to help her. The gun was for my protection in case something bad happened." She looked around. "Where is she? Inside the warehouse?"

Ian turned to the police officer. "This is Shannon Murphy. I can vouch for her. She's not one of the ones we're after. You can release her into my custody."

The officer shook his head again. But Ellison stepped forward. "Do as he says. Special Agent McKenzie can take custody of the gun and this young woman. I'll update Chief Thomas."

Ian winced at the use of his real name. Not that it really mattered at this point. His cover was blown.

"Where's Maria?" Shannon demanded as the police officer unlocked her handcuffs.

"Later," Ian snapped.

Her eyes widened, but she didn't say anything else.

Ian checked the loading on her pistol, his jaw tightening when he saw the magazine was full, except for one round. The officer had either ejected the chambered round or she hadn't chambered one herself. Thank God for small favors. He ejected the magazine and slid it into his pocket, then shoved the now-empty pistol in his other pocket.

"What's the status here?" Ellison asked, glancing from Nash to Ian.

Since the officer was still standing there, Ian glanced at his uniform to get his name. "Officer Jennings, thank you for your help tonight. Would you mind placing Miss Murphy in the back of your squad car until I can retrieve my personal car hidden down the mountain?"

The lot was rapidly filling as officers were driving each other to bring their squad cars out of hiding.

Jennings looked to Ellison for permission.

Ellison nodded. "If Chief Thomas comes looking for you, I'll let him know you're guarding a civilian on behalf of Homeland Security. Go ahead."

"Thank you, sir. My car's not here yet, but I'll borrow someone else's. No problem."

"I don't want to sit in the back of a police car," Shannon insisted. "I want to know what happened. Where's Maria?"

Ian noticed the panic in her expression. At any other time, her deep-seated fear of the police would have had him making some kind of concession. But not tonight. Her actions could have gotten her killed. And he needed to know, for sure, that she was safe.

"Home or the police station?" he gritted out. "Those are your choices."

Hurt flashed in her eyes. But she quickly covered it with a nonchalant expression as if she couldn't care less about what was going on.

Jennings took Shannon's arm and led her toward a patrol car near the tree line.

Ian deliberately turned his back on them, too incensed to even look at Shannon. It had almost destroyed him seeing her there, knowing that she could have been killed. Twice now, because of him, she'd been placed in an untenably dangerous situation. He wasn't sure what he was going to do about her. But that decision would have to wait.

"Give me the sitrep," Ellison demanded. "Chief Thomas said the warehouse is empty."

Ian narrowed his eyes and stepped forward, ready to let Ellison have it for ruining months of undercover work.

Nash moved between them, his back to Ellison. "Take a walk, Special Agent."

Ian gritted his teeth. "He ruined—"

"Take a walk. Now. I'll handle this."

Ian strode to the truck. He had too much adrenaline and anger running through his system to sit in the cab. Instead, he paced back and forth, waiting for the political grandstanding between agencies to end. That didn't seem like it would happen anytime soon since the Gatlinburg PD police chief had just joined the ADA and Nash.

Finally, disgusted with the whole thing, he decided to head back into the warehouse to see if maybe he'd missed something the first time around. Obviously, Butch and his men had been here recently to have placed that index card inside. Maybe they'd left something else lying around that could give him a clue about their current whereabouts.

He went in and headed straight for the room with the index card. He wanted a picture of it, if it hadn't been taken into evidence yet. A Gatlinburg PD evidence tech was placing the card into a clear evidence bag when Ian got there.

"Can I see that a second?" Ian pulled out his cell phone. "I'm the one who discovered it. I'd like a picture. It could help me with the investigation instead of waiting for the card to be processed."

The tech hesitated.

"Just hold it up," Ian said. "I won't touch the bag. No evidence chain of custody wrinkles here, okay?"

The man held it up, not looking happy about it.

Ian snapped a picture. "Thanks. Appreciate it." He turned to leave.

"Hey," the tech called out. "Don't you want a picture of the writing on the other side too?"

Ian slowly turned around. "There's writing on the back?"

The tech flipped it over. "Looks like it's addressed to somebody."

Ian's entire body went cold when he saw what was written there. He snapped the picture and kept his expression carefully blank. "Thanks. Does anyone else know about the writing on the back?"

He shrugged. "I doubt it. I'm pretty sure I was the first person to pick it up so it could be preserved for fingerprint analysis and testing of trace."

"No problem," Ian said, as if he was disappointed that the tech hadn't told anyone about it. "If you don't mind, I'll let the bosses know so they don't have to wait for processing. Is that okay?"

"Of course. It will save me the trouble of doing it. Thanks, Special Agent...um—"

"Savage." Ian nodded instead of offering to shake hands since the tech was still wearing gloves. The tech introduced himself, and Ian thanked him again for his assistance, then headed outside.

His boss was waiting for him when he reached the truck.

Nash frowned. "What were you doing inside?"

"Looking to see if anything useful was missed."

"Did you find anything?"

Ian shook his head. "Nope. What's our next step with the investigation?"

Nash snorted. "What investigation? It was all caught on camera. You were the inside guy to lure our traffickers into the open. That's all shot to heck now. We have nothing."

"We have suspects—Butch and his henchmen. We know they've been trafficking women. We just need proof."

"And how do you propose to get that now? It's over, Ian. I'm sorry, but that's the way it is. This one is a dead end. The bad guy is long gone—"

"We don't know that. Yes, my cover's

blown. But Butch could still be doing business here and looking for a new buyer. We can't give up. We need to keep digging, do some old-fashioned investigative work, maybe try to get another agent snooping around town undercover, posing as a buyer. We can't just wash our hands of this now. What will happen to those women? We have to keep working."

"*We* aren't doing anything on this. *I'll* evaluate what happened here tonight and figure out what, if anything, will be done. But I'm pulling most of the agents and sending them on other more promising cases. I'll keep a skeleton staff in town in case something else pops up. But if nothing does, we're out of here in the next few days."

"Nash, don't do this. Keep everyone on the case. We have to find where Butch is holding those women. Victims first, remember?"

Nash's face reddened. "I don't need you to keep reminding me about my job, Ian. This whole evening is a blight on both agencies. Ellison is all over me for not putting things on hold like we'd originally agreed. He insists that if we had, we could have had enough time to adequately plan the buy and nab these guys instead of the screwed-up situation at the last minute like we did today. And I can't even tell him he's wrong."

Ian started to argue, but Nash shook his head. "No. Not another word. Consider yourself on administrative leave for the next week. Make that two weeks. When you come back, I want your head on straight." He motioned toward the patrol car where Shannon was watching them through the back window. "And do something about Miss Murphy. I don't want her popping up in the middle of something if we do end up figuring out a way to salvage this mess."

Nash didn't give him a chance to argue further. He strode back to where the ADA and Chief Thomas were standing with some of the uniformed officers.

Ian stood there, mulling over what to do. He could try to argue with his boss again, but he didn't think it would do any good. And he wasn't sure he wanted to argue with him anyway, in light of what had been written on the back of the index card. He needed to think about his options and what to do next.

He glanced at the patrol car. Shannon looked away, refusing to meet his gaze. He let out a deep breath and pulled out his phone to bring up the picture of the card. He read the front, then flipped to the picture of the back. It contained six words.

For Homeland Security Agent Ian McKenzie.

Those six words, unbeknownst to the technician who'd collected the index card, canceled out everything written on the front. Those words meant that Butch had known that Ian was with Homeland Security, even before the swarm of cops and special agents descended on the warehouse. It was one thing for Butch to suspect he might be a cop. But Ian had made sure that only a few people had known that he was a special agent. That index card could only mean one thing.

Someone in law enforcement had tipped off Butch and his men, someone who knew that Ian worked for Homeland Security.

Chapter Thirteen

Ian pulled up his Charger in front of a small, remote mountainside hotel that looked down on the night lights of Gatlinburg.

In the passenger seat, Shannon stared mutinously ahead, arms crossed. "I've been safe at the duplex all these months that you've been living your double life. I still don't get why you suddenly think I'm in danger, especially since you said Butch and the others have most likely left town by now."

"Guys like him are unpredictable."

"Yeah, yeah, he's angry. Whatever."

He sighed. "Shannon, it's more serious than him simply being *angry*. He was expecting a big paycheck in exchange for off-loading what he calls inventory. Now he knows that Homeland Security and the local police are working together, looking for him. The heat is on, and he can't move easily with that many women in tow. It makes him vulnerable. He might even have to lie low here in town while he waits for things to cool down. That will cost him money. He'll blame me for that. He knows where I've been living. And Wolverine showed some interest in you the other day. He may decide to take revenge on me by hurting you."

"And that's why you had that other agent spying on me."

He dropped his hands to his lap. "Yes. As I already said, that's why Chris was there. Not that it did any good. You managed to slip right past him. Which is why I'm not taking you back there. Too many entrances and exits to watch. It's not safe."

"Right. Like you care." She shoved open the car door.

He reached across her and yanked the door shut. He was just inches from her face as she stared at him with her accusing green eyes.

"I do care, Shannon, or I wouldn't have put up with all of the cursing and hateful things you've been saying to me since I got you out of the patrol car."

She arched a brow. "You wouldn't have put up with it? What's that mean? You gonna hit me to prove how big and strong you are? *Cop?*"

He stared at her in shock. "You think I would hit you?"

"It wouldn't be the first time some guy I was hanging with beat the crap out of me."

"Then you've been hanging with the wrong men. I will never, ever hurt you. Never."

She stared at him, a disbelieving look on her face. "Right. You'll just take me prisoner instead. Isn't that called kidnapping or something? It's against the law. But I guess your fellow law enforcement buddies will cover for you. They always cover for each other, the brotherhood in blue."

"Good grief. You sure have a low opinion of me. Did I earn that tonight—because I wanted to protect you? Or have you felt that way a long time and have just done a really great job of hiding your true feelings?"

Her eyes widened. Then she quickly looked away, her mouth drawn into a tight line.

He let go of the door and sat back, but anchored her wrist with his hand before she could jump out of the car. "I didn't kidnap you. It's called protective custody. Whether you choose to believe it or not, there's a good possibility that your life is in danger. Until Butch and his men are caught, or I have definitive proof that they've left the area, you're staying with me. Unless you prefer a jail cell. Those are your choices."

"That's the second time you've threatened

to lock me up tonight. You getting kinky on me, Ian McKenzie?" She wiggled her brows, but the flash of anger in her eyes told the real story.

He shoved out of the car. It was either that or yell at her. Of all the lines that he'd crossed in his youthful rebel days, or even deep undercover pretending to be a thug, yelling at a woman—or worse—was a line he refused to cross.

He grabbed the small duffel bag from the back seat that Special Agent Chris Parker had brought to him from the duplex. A policewoman had packed items for Shannon while Chris had packed for Ian.

He settled the bag's strap over his shoulder and headed to the passenger side. For someone who'd been so adamant about getting out of the car earlier, Shannon seemed in no hurry to emerge now. He opened the door and stood back. "You coming, or are we driving to Gatlinburg PD?"

"If you give me my gun back, I can protect myself at the duplex."

"Not happening."

She rolled her eyes and got out.

Once they were inside their hotel suite she flounced into the bedroom and slammed the door.

Ian's shoulders slumped. He set the duffel bag on the little café table, took out his toothbrush and toothpaste and headed to the kitchenette in the corner. After changing into some warm-up pants and a T-shirt, he set the duffel bag outside the bedroom door.

"Shannon?" He waited, then rapped on the door. "Shannon, I've set the bag outside the door in case you need anything—"

The door opened. She grabbed the bag, then slammed the door closed.

He stared at the closed door for several long moments. But there wasn't anything he could think of to say that would make her overlook his biggest sin—that he was in law enforcement.

After making sure the locks were secure on the back window and only door into the suite, he checked the entry closet, hoping to find an extra pillow and a blanket. The closet was empty. He looked back at the couch, which was about two feet too short for him, then at the closed bedroom door. Sighing, he padded to the couch, lay down and drew his knees up against his chest.

Chapter Fourteen

Sleep was elusive for Shannon. She dozed off and on, but a combination of things kept waking her up. Not the least of which was guilt. She'd been awful to Ian. Her frustration and worry over her friend Maria, and her resentment at being forced to do something she didn't want to do, had her reverting to the smart-ass tough-girl persona she'd adopted in order to survive on the streets. But no matter how mean she was, and how angry Ian became, he'd been true to his word.

He hadn't hurt her.

And even though his high-handed insistence on taking her into protective custody had her panicking at the thought of giving control over to a man—*any* man—he'd proved time and again that he was only trying to help.

She'd seen the flash of regret on his face each time he'd forced her to do something she didn't want to do. And now that some time had passed, the panic and anger had faded enough for her to realize the truth. Ian didn't want to control her or force his will on her. He didn't want to hurt her and make her feel uncomfortable. He wanted only one thing—for her to be safe. And what had she done in return? She hadn't thanked him. Instead, she'd made every minute of the car ride—from the warehouse to the meeting with Chris to get the duffel bag and then finally to the hotel—a living hell for him.

And he didn't deserve that.

She sat up in the bed and threw off the covers. She'd finally met the genuinely nice, smart, sexy, sweet and protective man that she'd prayed would come into her life one day. And she'd done everything she could to turn him against her.

She was such an idiot.

She shuffled into the bathroom and freshened up. When she checked the time on her phone, she saw it was almost three in the morning. There was a light shining beneath the bedroom door. Maybe Ian was having trouble sleeping too. She owed him a huge apology. Might as well take care of it right now.

She pulled open the bedroom door, then felt lower than the lowest pond scum. There was big, brawny Ian looking like a pretzel, his long legs practically touching his chin on the short couch. She hadn't given a single thought to whether the furniture would accommodate his size before taking the king bed for herself. And since she'd shut the door that accessed the bathroom, he'd either been forced to go to the lobby to use their facilities, or hold it. Good grief, she was such a jerk. If he ever spoke to her again, it would be a miracle.

She knelt beside the couch and gently shook him.

His eyes flew open and he grabbed her, yanking her to the floor, crushing her beneath him as he swept his pistol back and forth toward the room around them. "What is it?" he demanded. "What happened?"

"Ian, it's just me." Her voice came out a harsh croak. She cleared her throat. "There's no one else here."

He frowned and looked down at her. "You're okay?"

She pressed shaking hands against his chest, an unexpected rush of tears clogging her throat. After everything she'd done, he was shielding her with his body, thinking someone was there to hurt her. He was willing to give his life for hers. The enormity of that knowledge had the tears flowing down her cheeks.

He shoved his pistol back into the holster and pulled her up with him, his concerned gaze searching hers. "I'm so sorry. I didn't mean to frighten you."

"Frighten me?" She laughed and wiped her tears. "You scared me nearly to death. But that's not why I'm crying. You shielded me with your body, trying to protect me, even after how badly I treated you."

His brow furrowed. "Are you sure you're okay? Did you hit your head?"

She laughed again. "No. I mean yes, I'm okay. I didn't..." She shook her head. "I'm fine. But you're not." She swept her hand toward the couch. "You shouldn't have let me keep the bedroom. This couch is way too small for you. And I was too stubborn and selfish to even think about that when I had my temper tantrum and went into the bedroom."

She grabbed his hand. When he winced, she let go, realizing she'd grabbed his left hand. "Oh, gosh. I'm so sorry. I forgot about your arm. Have you taken anything for the pain?"

He frowned. "I'm fine, Shannon. And I'm okay sleeping on the couch. Although if you have an extra pillow, I wouldn't turn it down."

"A pillow. Of course." She grabbed his other hand this time and tugged him toward the bedroom.

"Shannon—"

She pulled him into the bedroom. "Here you go. Four pillows, two for each of us. Plenty of room."

He stopped beside the bed and tugged his hand free. "Are you sleepwalking or something?" He waved a hand in front of her face.

She rolled her eyes. "I don't sleepwalk."

He glanced around the room. "Drunk, then? Did you hit the minibar?"

She put her hands on her hips. "I'm not asleep and I'm not drunk. I'm trying to be nice here."

He rubbed the back of his neck. "Yeah, that's the part that has me confused. I thought you hated me."

She narrowed her eyes at him.

"There we go. That's more like it." He grabbed a couple of pillows. "I'll be leaving now."

She stepped in his path, blocking his way to the door.

"Shannon?"

"Yes, Ian?"

"It's really late, or early by now. I could use a few more hours of sleep."

His eyes dipped down, then back up so fast she almost missed it. She was wearing a short nightshirt that barely fell below her hips. With no bra. And the bead of sweat trickling down the side of his neck told her he'd definitely noticed.

She took a step forward, her breasts pressing against his chest.

He swallowed, his gaze glued to hers. "Um, Shannon?"

"Yes, Ian?" She slid her arms up his biceps and locked her fingers behind his neck.

"I'm getting mixed signals here. Do you still, ah, hate me?"

She slowly shook her head. "I was mad, Ian. But I could never hate you. And I'm way past the mad stage. That's behind us now." She stroked the back of his neck.

He shuddered and briefly closed his eyes. "You know I'm still a cop, a special agent."

"That's your biggest flaw. I've decided to look past it." She stroked his neck again.

He stumbled, then swore and pulled her arms down from behind his neck. "I don't think this is a good idea. You're either overwrought or overtired or… Heck, I don't know. But you'll end up hating me later. Because that big flaw of mine is the core of who I am. Either you're okay with me being in law enforcement or you're not. Either you hate me or you don't. When you get it figured out, let me know. Until then, I think it's best that the door stays closed with you on one side and

me on the other. It's safer. For both of us."
He practically ran from the room, pulling the
door shut behind him.

Chapter Fifteen

Ian shoved the last of their breakfast trash into the garbage can beneath the kitchenette sink. The restaurant down the street that delivered to the tourist-rentals and hotels up this mountain had brought a delicious assortment of pancakes, eggs, bacon, and even oatmeal and fruit. But it had proved to be a waste. Neither of them seemed to have an appetite. And Shannon couldn't seem to even look at him since coming out of the bedroom this morning.

After barely eating anything, she'd thanked him politely, then planted herself on the couch in front of the TV to watch the morning news. Her thanking him was the longest conversation they'd had since last night's confusing drama in the bedroom. If he'd thought for one second that she truly wanted him, he'd have been all over her. But he hadn't trusted her motives, not after everything that happened yesterday. Seeing how she was acting this morning, he wasn't sure if he'd been right last night, or whether he'd made the biggest mistake of his life.

"Shannon?"

"Mmm-hmm." She didn't look at him.

"I'm about to leave now. Like I said, I'm going to follow up on a few things, see if anyone's making any headway trying to find out where Maria and the others might be."

He waited, then tried again. "If you're still upset about last night—"

"I'm fine."

He sighed. "I'll be back later today, definitely before dark. I've left cash on the counter so you can call that same restaurant that I called this morning to deliver any time you're hungry. Please don't use any of your credit cards or call anyone you know."

"You've said that three times now. I know the drill. And I know my choice is to stay here or go to jail. You can leave now. I'm not going anywhere."

He missed the easy friendship they'd shared for so long. Even the other night when he'd brought pizza by, and they'd watched that sappy love story, he'd rank that evening as one of the most enjoyable he'd ever had. He loved being with her, listening to her jokes, watching her face soften with emotion as she watched the actors on TV. How had they gone from that to this in such a short time?

"I said you could go now, Ian." She pushed the remote and changed the channel.

"You promise you won't go anywhere?"

"Cross my heart and hope to die," she said sarcastically.

"Then it should be okay to leave this with you." He set her pistol and the magazine on top of the counter.

She glanced over, then blinked. "You're giving me my gun back?"

"Is there a reason that I shouldn't? I can trust you. Right?"

She hesitated, then said, "Yes. Of course."

"There's no way for Butch or the others to know that you're here or even suspect it. But if a casual burglar were to decide to try to break in, or something like that, I want to know you'll be protected."

Her gaze finally lifted to his. "Thank you, Ian. I appreciate it."

He nodded. "I'll lock the door. But you'll need to throw the bar across it. Okay?"

"Okay." She smiled. "Be careful."

The smile surprised him, confused him. He didn't know what to make of it, so he just left.

Half an hour later he pulled up in front of the duplex. But instead of parking inside the garage, he left his Charger on the curb. Then he headed inside. Keeping all the lights off so no one could see him if they looked in from the street, he sat on the couch watching the car. Then he pulled out his cell phone and settled in to make some calls.

"Sanders Auto Repair. This is Ralph Sanders. Can I help you?"

"Boss, it's Ian."

"You'd better be on your way to the shop right now, Savage. Or you can kiss your job goodbye."

"Yeah, that's why I called. Partly, anyway." He explained who he really was and confessed that he'd been working there as a cover for the past six months. Convincing him would have been easier in person. But going to the shop today wasn't part of his plan.

"Well, I'll be a son of a… I can't believe it," Sanders finally said. "I mean, I do. But I gotta say, I'm mad as hell. Not that you were undercover all this time, but because I'm losing the best mechanic that I've ever had working for me. You sure you don't want to quit working for the Feds and come work for me full-time?"

Ian laughed. "The way things are going right now, I may need to take you up on that offer sometime. But not yet." Hopefully his boss at Homeland Security wouldn't fire him for working the case on his own when he was supposed to be on administrative leave. But he was playing with fire right now as far as his career was concerned.

"My door is always open, son. You did great work for me."

"Thank you, sir. I appreciate it. Since I've been gone, has anyone come around looking for me? They might not have come inside. They could be hanging around the place, maybe sitting in the lot across the street. One of them drives a white cargo van. Another drives a bright yellow Volkswagen, a fairly new Beetle. Seen anything like that parked outside the garage for no good reason?"

"Can't say that I've noticed. But we've been pretty slammed lately, and I've been pitching in working on the cars since my best worker ditched me."

Ian winced. "Sorry, sir."

"What makes you think I meant you?" Sanders laughed. "I'll check with the guys, keep an eye out. If I see this Bug hanging around, you want me to call you at this number?"

Ian was taking every precaution he could to ensure that nothing could be used to trace back to the hotel where he was keeping Shannon. That meant destroying his current burner phone as soon as today's work was done. Instead, he told Sanders that he'd call him back tomorrow to see if he'd found out anything that might help.

He called dozens of other contacts that he'd made in the time that he'd been working this investigation, including confidential informants willingly working in the sex trade. They claimed to enjoy what they did for a living, and since no one was technically forcing them, there wasn't much Ian could do other than to provide them a list of agencies, shelters and churches that made it their work to help sex trade workers. In return, his CIs provided him with tips.

As he made his calls, he kept a close watch on his car parked out front. But no one had even slowed down as they passed the duplex. No garish yellow Beetle pulled up behind the Charger. And even though he spoke to dozens of people in places where he'd gone in the guise of Ian Savage, no one claimed to have heard of anyone looking for him or asking questions about him. No one fitting Butch's description, or any of his minions, popped up on the radar.

It had been a long shot, but he was still surprised that everything was so quiet. He'd assumed that Butch or one of his right-hand men, or Wolverine at least, would have been out scouring the city trying to find the man who'd double-crossed them. He couldn't see them letting a slight like that go without wanting retribution. Either no one was searching for him, or they were driving yet another vehicle that he didn't know about. Or they'd left town already. Since that would mean the victims with Butch were completely beyond his reach and unlikely to be rescued, Ian was praying that wasn't the case.

While he worked through his contacts, he created a list of places he planned to canvass himself, places where his contacts weren't as likely to carry phones around. But at the top of his list was to start right where he was, in his current neighborhood. He wanted to see whether his neighbors had noticed anything suspicious. But before he could do that, there was one more call he needed to make.

He'd been putting this one off because he didn't want to make this call. But allowing his personal preferences to get in the way of solving a case and rescuing human trafficking victims was unacceptable. It was time to step up and get this particular chore over with. He dialed a number that he'd never used, even though it had been given to him years ago.

The line clicked. "McKenzie."

"Adam, it's Ian."

Chapter Sixteen

Shannon smoothed her blouse over her jeans, hesitating at the door to the hotel suite. She was breaking a promise by leaving. But Ian had lied to her for so long, it hardly seemed fair that she should feel so guilty over one little lie. And yet she did. He'd wanted her to stay here for her own protection. But how could she do that when the friend who'd risked her own life for her, a friend Shannon had spent much of her adult life tracking down, could be here somewhere in Gatlinburg at this very moment, in need of rescuing?

A car horn honked outside. The taxi she'd called was getting impatient. She took one last look around, then headed out the door.

Uncomfortable with the idea of sitting beside a driver she didn't know, she sat in the back seat.

He glanced at her in the rearview mirror. "Where to, ma'am?"

She gave him the duplex's address and brutally shoved her feelings of guilt aside. She knew the risks, that Butch or one of his men could be watching the place. But if she was going to pass as a street person again to try to hunt down news about Maria, she needed the right clothes for it. Her meager savings couldn't cover luxuries like a new outfit. Especially since her call this morning to let her boss know she was going to miss another shift had been short and *not* sweet. He'd fired her.

When the taxi pulled up in front of her home, she counted out the exact amount and handed it to the driver. He didn't look happy to not be getting a tip. But she couldn't afford one, and she refused to use Ian's equally hard-earned money when she was going against his wishes.

The taxi's tires squealed as he took off, making her wince as she turned the key in the lock. After one last glance around to make sure that she didn't see anyone skulking in the bushes or parked on the street watching her, she headed inside.

IAN ADJUSTED the collar of his leather trench coat, since his favorite leather jacket had been destroyed, and headed inside the internet café. He immediately spotted his oldest brother. Adam was doing his best to blend in, having chosen a table in the back corner away from the busy counter. But McKenzies, because of their large build and height, were more likely to be noticed than not. Ian imagined the thousand-dollar suit that Adam was wearing, along with his coal-black hair and striking blue eyes, didn't help. But he seemed oblivious to all the women casting glances his way.

Adam motioned toward him. Ian returned the greeting and headed to his table. He couldn't help grinning when he noticed that he had the opposite effect on the women around them. His blond-streaked spiky black hair and dragon tattoos must not be to their taste.

"Something funny?" Adam asked, looking puzzled.

Ian shrugged. "Nothing I'm not used to. Thanks for meeting me here."

"Not a problem." He gestured toward Ian's face. "The bruises are fading fast. How's the arm?"

"Nothing a few pain pills don't knock out. You said you have information on Gillespie?"

The disappointment on Adam's face told Ian he'd messed up, again. His brother must have wanted more small talk, to catch up on a personal level before turning to business. Ian was too out of practice with polite conversation to realize it.

Ian cleared his throat. "How's, ah, your new bride? Jody, I think you said?"

Adam smiled sadly. "Thanks for the effort. But you're obviously in a hurry, so I'll get right to the point of our meeting." He pulled a manila folder out of the briefcase on the seat beside him and set it on the table in front of Ian. "You can take those with you. I just got the information together this morning and haven't had a chance to digitize it. It's a good thing you called."

"This stuff wasn't already in Memphis PD's computer databases?"

"I imagine it is. But my former partner grew up in the days of typewriters and legal pads. I doubt he even went online in the department's system to gather this information. He probably got it from the archive paper backups in the basement and made copies. At least he sent it overnight instead of your typical snail mail, or we still wouldn't have it." He pointed to one of the reports as Ian thumbed through the pages. "That's an overview of the investigation into the sex ring I told you about."

"What are all these? Surveillance photographs?" Ian began sifting through a stack of pictures.

"Most of them, yes. They were taken in the months and weeks before we did our sting. Others are mug shots of the guys we arrested." He pulled one of them from beneath a few others and set it on top. "That's your guy there, Gillespie."

Ian frowned and held up the picture. "How long ago was this?"

"A little over two years." He flipped the photo over and grinned. "Two years, three weeks and two days, to be exact." He tapped the handwriting on the back. "That's my old partner's work." He handed it back to Ian.

"He sure has bulked up since then. I almost don't recognize him."

"Yeah, well, as I'm sure you know in your line of work, these guys do everything they can to change their appearance when they start over somewhere else. They don't want anyone from their old life to spot them. Every indication is that he left Memphis shortly after that mug shot was taken and the charges against him didn't stick."

"When I was in the hospital, I remember you saying something about his right-hand men, that they went to prison. Were you able to verify that they're still locked up?"

Adam held his hand out for the pictures. "May I?"

Ian gave the stack to him and Adam fanned them out. He selected three and set them in front of Ian. "These are the main guys, the ones giving the orders. All three are serving time as we speak. But everyone in our task force believed Gillespie was the brains behind the operation. He had everyone too scared to turn on him and testify against him. It killed me that we had to let him walk."

"Okay, well, I'll look through all of this, study Gillespie's background. If I can figure out where he's been, maybe I can find out where he's going. Maybe some of these smaller fish caught in your net are out and working with him again. I can follow up that angle, as well."

"What about your fellow agents at Homeland Security? They helping you with this?"

Ian grimaced. "Not officially. I called a few I trust this morning to discuss the investigation."

"A few you trust? You don't trust everyone you work with?"

He wasn't quite ready to discuss all the particulars with his brother. This new truce, or whatever it was between them, wasn't something he was comfortable with just yet. So he didn't tell him about the index card and his suspicions about a mole.

"I wouldn't say that. But I'm on administrative leave right now. My cover was blown, so I'm officially off the investigation. Any snooping I do, if it's reported up to my boss, won't be good for my career. I'm being careful about whom I contact on the inside right now."

"I see."

The disappointment on Adam's face had Ian tensing. This was what he normally expected from his brothers rather than the friendly cooperation of a moment before. They expected him to fail, to screw up everything. So naturally Adam assumed the worst. Never mind that Ian had done everything right, everything by the book, and it was someone else who'd blown his cover.

He gathered up all the pictures and reports and slid them back into the folder. "Thanks, Adam. I really appreciate this." He pushed his chair back.

"Ian?"

He arched a brow in question.

"Christmas is in three weeks."

"Yeah. What about it?"

Adam frowned. "You missed Thanksgiving—"

"I usually miss Thanksgiving." He didn't

want to feel like a hypocrite sitting around the table trying to come up with something to say when it was his turn to say why he was thankful. Not having to see his father every day didn't seem appropriate.

"You missed my wedding in June. I posted the information in the paper and sent an invitation to your PO box and—"

"I was undercover. It would have been too risky to be seen at an event like that, especially here in Gatlinburg. And, honestly, I haven't checked that PO box in ages. I have to admit that I didn't know about the wedding." He'd rented that box at his family's insistence years ago and put it on automatic renewal. But he rarely ever checked it.

Adam held up his hands in a placating gesture. "I get it. But you said your cover has been blown now, that you're off the case, at least officially. It sure would be great if you could be there for Duncan's and Colin's weddings at Christmas. The ceremony will be at one in the converted barn at the family cabin. It would mean a lot to Mom if you're there. It would mean a lot to all of us."

Ian snorted in disbelief.

"I'm serious, Ian. We want you there."

"Including Dad?"

Adam hesitated.

"That's what I thought." Ian stood and held up the manila folder. "I really appreciate this. It could be the break I need."

Adam stood, as well. "Enough to repay me by showing up at the weddings?"

It was Ian's turn to hesitate. He had planned on being there Christmas morning for his mother's sake. Easter and Christmas were her favorite holidays, and he always tried to be at one of them every year. But pretending he was part of a big happy family at something like a wedding left a sour taste in his mouth. Still, his brother had never asked him for anything before. That alone had him holding back a quick no. "What are their names? Colin's and Duncan's fiancées?"

"Duncan's marrying someone from Colorado, a former FBI agent, Remi Jordan."

"And Colin?"

"Peyton Sterling."

Ian stared at him in shock. "Her arsonist sibling nearly killed Colin. The fire—"

"I know. Some crazy stuff happened this year. I'd like to bring you up to speed, when you have time."

Ian couldn't seem to process what his brother had just said. How could Colin forgive and then propose to the woman who'd supposedly loved him, then abandoned him in a burn unit to support the man responsible for putting him there? That had to be a hell of a story.

"Ian? Will you do it? Will you come to the weddings?"

Ian shrugged, then winced and made a mental note to take another pain pill once he got to his car. "I'll think about it. No promises."

Adam nodded. "I can't ask for more than that, all things considered. Thanks, Ian."

The brother Ian was used to would have argued with him, maybe even berated him for being a rebel, the bad boy who continued to bring disgrace to the McKenzie name. Marriage must have mellowed him. Maybe Duncan and Colin would be easier to get along with too, after they got married. But that was probably too much to hope for.

Ian left without another word.

In his car in the lot behind the building, he swallowed some pain pills. Then he took out the contents of the folder again. A name had caught his attention on one of the reports. Sure enough, when he looked again, he saw it—Cameron Ellison. He'd been an assistant district attorney in Memphis before transferring to Gatlinburg. The DA who Ellison reported to worked out of Memphis, not Gatlinburg. It was an odd setup. And it was a change in location, not a change in jobs. So why was Ellison here? Was it temporary on some special assignment, and he just happened to also be given the role of liaison with Homeland Security for the current human trafficking investigation? Or was there a more sinister reason for his transfer? Ian couldn't help thinking about that yellow index card in the warehouse. Was Ellison the one who'd ratted him out to Gillespie?

It was definitely an angle he'd have to explore. He sorted through the pictures again, remembering one that had caught his eye in the café. It was a mug shot. The inmate had terrible taste in clothing. His black-and-yellow shirt made him look like a bumblebee. The information on the back of the picture said the perpetrator was a suspected low-level member of the organization. But there hadn't been enough evidence to hold him over for prosecution, just as there hadn't been for Gillespie. They'd both been released at the same time. The man's name was Andrew Branum.

But Ian knew him as Wolverine.

Now that he knew Wolverine's real name, maybe it was time to dig a little and find out what else he was hiding.

Ian pulled out his phone and made a call.

Chapter Seventeen

Having traveled from her hometown in Ohio to both Virginias, Kentucky and now Tennessee, Shannon had lived in so many small towns and big cities that she'd lost track of them all. But one thing was the same in every place she'd been—a part of town where extreme poverty, homelessness and people who wanted to make a profit no matter what the human cost came together to cause misery and destroy lives.

Shannon had been one of the victims of that world for over five years, since the age of fourteen. And even though she'd escaped "the life" a few years ago, it was depressingly easy to slip back into that role, as if she'd never managed to claw her way out of it. Except this time, she wasn't anyone else's property. And she wasn't defenseless.

She kept her right hand firmly on the bulge of the pistol in her purse as she navigated back alleys in a pair of red stilettos, a black leather miniskirt and an off-the-shoulder short crimson blouse that allowed the sunlight to sparkle off her belly ring. Her only concession to the chilly temperatures was the waist-length leopard-print jacket that she kept unbuttoned as any good street girl would. After all, you couldn't make a sale if you didn't advertise the goods.

Back on either River Road or Parkway, she'd have stuck out like a black bear in a herd of elk. But here on the outskirts, she blended right in. Which was exactly what she wanted.

Business was slow this early in the day. But there were still a few johns idling on the curbs, negotiating prices with achingly young women leaning into their windows, displaying their cleavage in the hopes of bumping up the prices. As Shannon approached, one of the women hopped into a car and was driven away. The bleakness in her eyes as she looked out the window tugged at Shannon's heart, and reminded her of herself not long ago, when she'd been forced into the same kind of life.

Tears burned the backs of her eyes as she stepped over a homeless man huddled beneath his cardboard house, covered in piles of dirty blankets. If she thought her jacket would come even close to fitting him, she'd have given it to him. As it was, she couldn't walk past him without stopping to stuff one of her few remaining twenty-dollar bills into his hand.

Hurrying past him before his fervent thank-yous made someone wonder if she had more cash on her, she turned down another side street. Perhaps sensing that she was the real deal, or at least had been at one time, the women on the curbs and sheltering in doorways weren't alarmed about her inquiries. They seemed to genuinely want to help her find her "big sister, Maria." It would have been much easier if she'd had a picture to show them. But with Maria's striking Spanish looks and the butterfly tattoo on her neck, it was easy to provide a useful description.

Several of the women claimed to have seen Maria. But every lead that Shannon followed took her to another woman or the occasional pimp out checking on his ladies. And none of them led to her friend.

After several hours of walking the streets, her feet were starting to ache and burn, which surprised her. She wore high heels every day as part of being a hostess at the hotel restaurant. But the stilettos stretched her arches and cramped her toes in a way her every-day heels didn't. If she couldn't find anyone with knowledge of Maria's whereabouts soon, she'd have to call it a day.

She glanced around before dipping her hand into her purse to check the time on her phone. It was even later than she'd realized. If she didn't get back to the hotel soon, Ian might very well make it back before her. That was a conversation she didn't want to have. It was time to give up, at least for now.

She turned the corner to make her way back toward the more respectable part of town, where she'd be more likely to find a taxi. She'd just passed a darkened doorway when movement out of the corner of her eye sent alarm skittering up her spine. She shoved her hand into her purse for her gun and tried to whirl around. The man behind her grabbed her wrist, his other arm going around her waist. She screamed as he yanked her back toward the darkened doorway.

He grabbed the gun out of her hand, then immediately let her go.

Shannon whipped around, ready to destroy his chances of fathering children with one swift kick of her stiletto. But the moment she turned, she froze. The man dressed in black looking down at her with fury in his deep blue eyes wasn't a stranger.

"I-Ian? What are you doing here?"

He ejected the magazine in her pistol and cleared the chamber before giving them both back to her. "I was speaking to confidential informants, searching for clues to help me rescue your friend and the women with her. But I had to stop all that when I heard about a woman with blue-tipped black hair making a stir. You about done here?"

His words were short and clipped, his anger so palpable it made goose bumps rise on her arms.

"Yes, actually. I was about to find a taxi."

His jaw tightened. "A taxi. That's how you got here?"

"Well, you didn't exactly leave me a car. What was I supposed to do?"

A muscle started to tick in the side of his cheek. "Keeping your word and staying at the hotel would have been good for a start." He flicked the collar of her leopard-print jacket. "I seem to remember something like that in your closet. You went to the duplex?"

"Well, I couldn't exactly blend in around here in my normal clothes. I had to get a different outfit. But I was careful. I had my gun."

His nostrils flared as if he was having trouble drawing enough oxygen. He motioned toward the next corner. "My car is that way." He didn't wait for Shannon. Instead, he stalked down the sidewalk away from her.

Stubbornness and pride wanted her to refuse his implied order that she follow him. But she wasn't going to waste her precious store of cash on another taxi just to make a point, and she was ready to return to the hotel anyway. She started after him, hurrying to catch up. By the time she rounded the corner, she was limping. How had she survived so many years wearing these stupid shoes?

Ian, in spite of the anger darkening his expression, couldn't seem to ignore the gentlemanly manners that had always set him apart from other men she'd known. He stood with the passenger door open, waiting for her.

She got inside and soon they were whipping through back streets, making their way up the mountain toward the hotel. She kept expecting him to berate her, yell at her, something. Instead, he didn't say a word.

By the time they reached the hotel, she was so relieved to escape the tense atmosphere inside the car that she shoved out of her door before he'd even put the car in Park. Once she was in the main room, she drew a deep breath and turned around to explain. Ian strode right past her into the bedroom.

Was he going to lock her out? Make her take the couch in retaliation for last night? It was close to dinnertime, not quite bedtime. What was he doing? She stepped to the door, and was almost run down when he shoved past her with the duffel bag. He held the main door open and stared at the far wall, waiting.

"I guess we're switching hotels?" she said.

"Something like that."

"Why? I thought this place was supposed to be safe."

He finally looked at her. "Did the taxi that you took to the duplex pick you up here?"

She blinked as his words sank in. If someone had been watching the duplex as Ian suspected, and saw her arrive in the cab, they could have bribed the driver—the one she hadn't tipped—to tell them where he'd picked her up. All of Ian's careful measures, like driving in circles and constantly looking in his mirrors to ensure that no one followed them in his car, were for nothing. She'd just left a bread-crumb trail for Butch and the others to follow directly to the hotel, if they were truly looking for her and Ian.

She cleared her throat. "Ian, I'm sorry. I just wanted to look for Maria and—"

He motioned toward the open door.

She straightened her shoulders and marched outside.

After what seemed like an eternity because of how meticulous Ian was about making sure they weren't followed, Ian slowed on the winding mountain road and turned into a driveway. In front of them was an enormous two-story log cabin. It was the biggest cabin she'd ever seen. Mansion seemed like a more appropriate label for something that huge.

He pulled into the three-car garage and cut the engine. Once the door was closed, he got out and led her into the main house.

Her jaw dropped open when she saw the interior. Thick golden logs crisscrossed two stories above to support the wide-open space inside. A one-of-a-kind hand-hewn log railing formed an interior balcony that looked down over the massive great room. And at the far end, a wide staircase with more log railings and stone steps soared up to the balcony, leading to several doors off both ends of the house, presumably the bedrooms.

"This is incredible," she breathed. "Whoever owns it must be a bajillionaire. Whose place is it?"

"Mine."

Chapter Eighteen

Ian strode through the monstrosity of a cabin, giving Shannon the grand tour as she padded barefoot behind him, her stilettos discarded near the front door. At first, he was still so shaken and livid over her risking her life yet again that it didn't bother him one bit that she was silent as he showed her the downstairs. She simply nodded when he gave her the security alarm code, and later explained how to work the remote controls for the wall of electronics built into the stone ledges beside the two-story fireplace. But as the tour went on, and she still didn't say anything, his anger began to fade and concern took its place.

Beside the marble-topped kitchen island that overlooked the great room, he turned to face her. "I have people come up here once a week to clean and perform any required maintenance inside and out. But since I'm rarely ever here myself, there's nothing to eat.

There are some bottles of water in the refrigerator, but that's pretty much it. What do you want for dinner? I can have something delivered."

She shook her head. "No, thank you. I'm not really hungry."

He studied her pale complexion, the shadows in her eyes. "Did you eat lunch?"

"I'm fine. Really. I just…"

"You just what?"

She shrugged. "I wonder why you think we'll be safe here. Can't Butch search the internet for your name and find this address?"

"No one is going to find us here. The deed isn't under my real name."

"Because of your job?"

"Because of my family. They don't know I have this place, and I'd prefer it stay that way."

Her eyes widened. Then she looked away. "I'm a little tired. If you don't mind, I'd like to lie down."

When she still wouldn't look at him, he sighed and turned around. "I'll show you the bedrooms. They're all upstairs." He grabbed the duffel bag that he'd left in the great room and led the way up the curved staircase to the second-floor balcony. At the top, he motioned to the right. "There are some guest rooms down there. More here in the middle. The master's at the other end."

"Does it matter which room I take?"

He shook his head. "They each have their own bathroom. Clean towels and sheets are in the linen closets."

She stepped into the guest room that was the closest to where they were standing. "This will be fine. Thank you." She moved past the king-size bed, lightly running her hands across the deep blue duvet before turning around.

Ian set the duffel bag on top of the mahogany dresser and took out the smaller bag inside that held his things, plus the manila folder that Adam had given him. He waved toward one of the doors. "The bathroom should have everything you need—shampoo, soap, hair dryer. But if you think of something else you want, let me know. I'll—"

"Call someone and have it delivered?"

He frowned at her strained tone, but nodded. "If you're worried that it's not safe to have someone deliver something, don't. Nothing's—"

"In your name. Got that." She wrapped her arms around her middle and glanced around the room.

Ian waited, but when she didn't say anything else, he turned to leave.

"I guess Homeland Security pays really well these days."

He stopped, then slowly turned around. "Is there something you want to ask me, Shannon?"

She pierced him with an accusing look and motioned to encompass the room. "Cops can't afford places like this. Please tell me you won the lottery."

He stiffened, his earlier anger surging through him again. But this time it wasn't because she could have gotten herself killed. "I don't play the lottery."

She stared at him, waiting. "Are you going to make me say it?"

"Yeah. I guess I am."

She sighed. "I thought you were one of the good ones, Ian. How can you afford a mansion? One you don't even live in?"

He breathed through the anger and the disappointment, not answering until he was sure he could speak without yelling. "Of all the people I've met in my life, only one made me feel accepted for who I am, inside. She didn't judge me, condemn me for the choices I'd made in my life. She judged me on my character, on how I acted, on how I treat other people. Until the past few days, and right now."

Her eyes widened.

"This stupid cabin was my first rebellious act after I came into my first million when I turned twenty-one—the day my father turned over my inheritance to me. He was certain I'd waste the money, so of course that was the first thing I did—built a house I hated from day one and have never lived in for more than a few days at a time. I realized the stupidity of building this place as soon as it was finished. I never told my family about it, because I didn't want to give them proof that they were right."

She started to say something, but he held up a hand to stop her. "The money came from my great-great-grandfather, passed down through the generations. He was a genius in the business world. By the time he passed away, he was a multimillionaire a dozen times over. And that's not even in today's money. He'd have been a billionaire if you account for inflation."

"Ian, I'm sorry. I shouldn't have—"

"No. You shouldn't have." He rubbed the back of his neck, then dropped his hand to his side. "I don't know why you keep comparing me to the scumbags of your past. Cop or not, I'd do anything it takes to protect you. I don't want to die for you, Shannon. But if someone points a gun at you, I'll be the first one to jump in front of it."

He stepped out the door, then looked back over his shoulder. "You've always worried that others would judge you because of your past. That they would think less of you for it. I've never done that. I see you for the victim you once were, the survivor you've become. And yet, the moment you find out that I'm in law enforcement, you judge me. You think the worst of me in spite of everything else you know about my character." He motioned to encompass the room as she'd done a few minutes earlier. "I have more money than my future grandchildren's children could ever spend, and yet I risk my life every day on the streets. I do it because I want to help people. I want to make a difference in this world. And you know what? I'm done apologizing for it."

He stalked out the door and didn't stop until he was downstairs in his office, on the opposite side of the house.

Chapter Nineteen

The smell of pizza wafted up from down-stairs about an hour later. Shannon didn't bother going down to have some even though she knew Ian would have ordered enough to share. She didn't deserve anything from him, not after how she'd acted. Not that she was planning on going on a hunger strike. A girl had to eat. But she'd wait, give him time to go back to his office or wherever he'd gone earlier, so he didn't have to look at her across the table while he ate.

She'd been so horrible to him.

Everything he'd said was true. He'd never judged her on her past. Not once. He'd never raised his voice to her, even when he was furi-ous as he'd been earlier this evening. And she had no doubt that he was telling her the truth now, about everything. She knew his charac-ter. He was right about that. She knew more about him than his own family in many ways, things he'd told her about his past, about why he didn't have a relationship with his father and barely spoke to his brothers. That if it wasn't for his mom, whom he loved dearly, he'd never go back home for his infrequent visits. And yet, when she'd been put to the test, instead of believing the best of him—as she should have—she'd proved she was no better than his judgmental father.

She really hated herself right now.

But if she could do it over, and she was honest with herself, she'd have done it the same way. She'd have asked the same questions, said the same things. Because even though she knew in her heart that he was the best person she'd ever met, probably ever would, the difficult lessons of her past continued to rear their ugly heads. The fear that something would happen, that if she and Ian were actually together as a couple one day, he'd destroy all her illusions. He'd hit her, hurt her, turn into the ugly, angry kind of person all of the men in her life had eventually become.

It wasn't fair, to either of them, that she had this irrational fear. But there it was. And she had no idea how she'd ever move past it. Maybe if Ian ever really took a bullet for her, that would destroy her unreasonable fears.

And wasn't that a horrible thought? The awful scene between them tonight had been fate intervening. Fate was protecting Ian from the kind of life he might have if they were ever really together. Her mama and all her "daddies" had really messed her up. Ian deserved someone who wasn't damaged goods. He deserved someone supportive, someone who realized how wonderful he was and didn't look at him with doubt, and wonder when the fairy tale would fall apart.

Several hours had passed before she crept down the stairs to stop the growling in her stomach. The house, or at least this part of the massive structure, was dark, lit only by the moonlight in the floor-to-ceiling wall of glass that framed the fireplace.

Assuming Ian was asleep in the master bedroom upstairs, she was as quiet as she could be and didn't turn on any lights. She grabbed a bottle of water and two pieces of pizza from the refrigerator. Whoever had brought the pizza last night must have brought groceries too, because there was fresh milk, eggs and dozens of other items that hadn't been there earlier.

Not wanting to risk the ding of the microwave waking Ian, she sat at the island to eat her slices cold. When she took her first bite and realized the pizza was pepperoni, bacon, extra sauce and extra cheese, the tears started rolling down her face.

She dropped the pizza to the paper towel that she was using as a plate and covered her mouth to keep her sobs of anguish from being heard.

The lights flickered on overhead. Ian stood near the other end of the massive island, still wearing the jeans and navy-blue T-shirt he'd been wearing earlier. He must have been in his office this whole time. His brows furrowed with concern. "Are you okay?"

"Am I okay?" She laughed without humor and swiped at the tears on her face. "How awful do I have to be to you before you stop being so nice to me? I don't deserve your concern. You should hate me by now."

His expression turned sad as he shook his head. "It would be impossible for me to hate you, Shannon." He crossed to the countertop and grabbed a stack of napkins, then set them down in front of her. "Why are you crying? Is it Maria? I haven't given up trying to find her. I've been working on the investigation all evening. Not that I have much to show for it. But I'm doing everything I can. And my guys tell me they're still following up on leads, as well."

She dropped one of the napkins on top of her pizza, her appetite gone. "Maria. Here I am feeling sorry for myself, not even thinking about my friend. And you've been up all night working to find her. How can you stand the sight of me?"

He moved to stand beside her bar stool, smiling down at her. "Oh, I don't know. From where I stand, you look pretty good."

"I'm serious, Ian."

"So am I." He leaned his hip against the island. "And I haven't been up all night. It's only a little past nine, Grandma."

His good-natured teasing had her smiling in spite of herself. "How do you do it?"

"Do what?"

"You can always make me smile, no matter how bleak things look. I don't deserve to have you for a friend, assuming we're still friends?" She couldn't help the desperately hopeful note in her voice.

He cupped her face and pressed a whisper-soft kiss against her lips, then stepped back. "Friends. Always. If you can forgive my rotten disposition earlier. I shouldn't have gone off on you like that."

"Stop it. Please. Just stop. I'm the one who should apologize—"

"Apology accepted, as long as you agree to

eat more than a few bites. Here." He retrieved her pizza from beneath the napkin and put it on a plate. "I'll nuke it for you. Don't forget that I know your worst secrets, like that you hate cold pizza." He shoved it into the microwave.

"You definitely know my worst secrets."

He set the now-warm pizza slices in front of Shannon and took the bar stool beside her. "I think we're even on that score. No more secrets between us. No more lies. Friends should be able to trust each other and count on each other. Deal?"

"I don't deserve you, Ian."

"We're even on that score too. I don't deserve you either. Do we have a deal?"

She smiled and held up her hand. "Pinkie swear."

He grinned and hooked his finger around hers. "Pinkie swear. And don't ever tell anyone else that I did that. They'll take my man card."

"I'll keep that information in my back pocket in case I ever need to force you to do my bidding."

He laughed, and just like that, it was as if all the hurt of the last few hours had never happened. But it had. And she knew that until she could learn to let go of her fears, if that was even possible, that there was no hope of a permanent future between them. Not the kind of future she'd dreamed about at least. Before finding out that he was a special agent for Homeland Security, she'd thought she'd found her perfect partner. She loved his tattoos. He loved hers. He found her belly ring sexy. And his blond-streaked black hair made her blue-tipped hair seem almost conventional.

"Note to self," he said. "Lose that joke. It fell flat."

She blinked. "Sorry. I was kind of lost in thought."

"Something more important than listening to my jokes?"

She smiled and grabbed for the first thing that came to mind. She certainly wasn't going to tell him that she was fantasizing about his tattoos and what might have been. "Earlier you said you hate this house. It's beautiful. And not pretentious like you might expect from something this big. It has a homey feel to it."

He looked around as if trying to see it through her eyes. "I guess so. Saying I hate it might be an overstatement. I hate the idea of it, of my rebellious folly just to spite my father. It's a ridiculous waste of money, way too big for one person. And since I'm out of town or out of state most of the time, deep undercover a lot of times, I'm never here. I really should sell it."

"Hmm. Maybe. It would be perfect for a large family. I can see kids sitting around the stone hearth roasting marshmallows in the fireplace. Or catching lightning bugs outside."

"Shannon Rose Murphy, when did you become so conventional? The next thing I know, you'll be wanting a white picket fence and to join the PTA."

She shoved him good-naturedly. "Just because I'm not conventional doesn't mean I wouldn't like to have a family and a nice house someday—minus the picket fence, of course."

"Of course." He tilted his head, studying her. "I can see it. I bet you'd be a great mom. How many kids does future Shannon want?"

She blinked, surprised to feel tears starting in her eyes again.

His smile faded. "Shannon, what—"

She held her hands up to stop him. "It's stupid. I'm sorry. I just… The idea of really having kids is…" She drew a shaky breath. "I never knew who my dad was. He could have been any number of men in and out of my mother's life. And there wasn't a maternal bone in her body. All I was good for was cleaning our run-down apartment or, later, turning tricks to help put food on the table. I'm damaged goods all the way around. No one would want me to be the mother of their children. I'm sure I'd do something to screw them up for life, just like my mom did to me." She hopped off the bar stool. "I'll clean up my mess in here later. I just want to go to bed now. Good night, Ian."

She'd just reached the stairs when he stepped in front of her, blocking her way. He didn't say anything. Instead, he opened his arms. She sobbed and threw herself against him. Then he was lifting her and cradling her in his arms against his chest.

"Ian, stop. Your hurt arm," she protested between tears as he carried her up the stairs.

"You weigh less than a feather. Don't worry about my arm."

She laid her head against him, the feel of his chest beneath her cheek, his arms tight around her so wonderful she quit protesting. He kissed the top of her head and whispered soothing words as he took her into the guest bedroom. A quick dip and he'd raked the covers back. Then he settled her onto the sheets and tucked the covers up around her.

The loss of his touch had her crying again.

Being held by him had felt so right, so perfect, as if that was where she belonged.

He gently swept her hair back from her face, his deep blue eyes filled with concern. And something else. His gaze heated as he stared down at her, his fingers growing still in her hair. His Adam's apple bobbed in his throat, and he straightened away from the bed. "I'd better go."

She grabbed his hand and threaded their fingers together. "You don't have to. You can stay. I *want* you to stay."

"I don't think that's a good idea." He tugged his hand free and strode toward the door.

"Ian, wait." She slid off the bed and stopped in front of him by the balcony outside the guest room. "We've kissed too many times for you to tell me that you don't want me. And I seem to remember you proving to me not long ago that you wanted me very much." She pressed her hand against his chest, then slid it down.

He swore and grabbed her hand, then drew a ragged breath. "Wanting you isn't the problem. It's about doing what's right."

"We're two consenting adults. Unless you're saving yourself for marriage or something."

He laughed and pushed her hand away. "It's a little late for me to save myself."

"Well, we both know I never got the chance to save myself for marriage." She grimaced. "Is that it?" She swallowed and took a step back, pressing a hand to her throat. "Oh my gosh. That's it, isn't it? It's because of my past. You say you don't care, that you don't judge me. But when it comes to the idea of getting naked with me, you're disgusted, aren't you? Because of all those men—"

His eyes flashed with anger, but somehow, she knew the anger wasn't directed at her. He pulled her against him and cupped her face. "Don't ever think that. Nothing that happened to you is your fault. And none of it could make me think any less of you in any way. You're sexy and smart and funny and…" He shook his head. "It's not about your past. It's about who we are and what we want." He pressed his hand over his heart. "What drives me is my passion for law enforcement. But the very idea of that frightens you. I don't think we could ever move past that."

She frowned. "I'm not asking you to marry me, Ian. I'm not talking about forever. I'm talking about one night."

His hands shook as he cupped her face again and searched her eyes. "Aren't you? I heard the catch in your voice when you talked about having a home, children. I've held myself back all the time we lived in the duplex because there were lies between us. It wouldn't have been right for me to sleep with you while I was hiding the fact that I was a cop—the one thing you hate most. And now that you know the truth, I'm still what you fear. Admit it. You can't trust me."

She started to deny it, but all the hurts and pain of her past made her hesitate. By the time she was able to gather her scattered thoughts again, he'd already dropped his hands. She hated herself in that moment.

He smiled sadly. "Even if we didn't have that between us," he continued, "you hunger for a stable home, for everything you were denied while growing up. I've had that—a mom who loved me, a dad I loved and who loved me back until we had our falling-out. My times with my brothers weren't all bad either. There were a lot of good times. But when I turned seventeen, everything changed. You know why."

"Willow."

He nodded. "Everything changed after that. I changed. I don't want the house and the picket fence and babies. I want freedom to move every few months, to start a new investigation. If I was married, I couldn't do that. I wouldn't do that. It wouldn't be right.

I'd settle down, build a life. But I'd be miserable doing it. And that's not a recipe for a successful marriage. So, no, I won't make love to you, Shannon. Even though I want to, so much sometimes I feel like I'll die if I don't."

She fisted her hands and stared up at him. "I don't understand how everything you said means that we can't make love."

"Don't you?" He searched her gaze. "You still haven't figured it out?"

She shook her head. "No. You're completely confusing me."

He shut his eyes for a moment, then blew out a long, slow breath before looking at her again. "I'm in love with you, Shannon. Hopelessly, head over heels in love with you."

Her mouth dropped open in shock.

He laughed bitterly. "I've done a really good job of hiding that. But it's true. And if I take you to my bed, and then have to let you go, I don't know that I could survive. And since I know there's no way that I can make you happy, even if you could look past the fact that I'm a special agent, a future between us isn't even in the realm of possibilities. It's better that we stay friends. Very good friends. And after this case is resolved, you go your way and I go mine. You'll eventually find a man who can give you everything you want, someone who will treat you like a queen and give you babies and a home and who will be there every day. But I'm not that man." He kissed her on the top of her head, then slowly walked away.

Chapter Twenty

What did a girl wear when she was going to see the man who'd told her the night before that he was in love with her? Then promptly rejected her and walked away? Should she pay extra attention to her makeup and hair to tempt him to change his mind? Or should she do herself up to salvage her wounded ego? Whatever the real reason, she fussed over her makeup and hair far longer than usual. And now she stood contemplating which top to wear with her jeans. The red one or the blue one—the only two blouses she had that were clean.

Telling herself it didn't matter since Ian only wanted to be friends, she threw on the red top. Then she changed her mind because it clashed with the blue tips of her hair and put on the blue blouse. Then she cursed herself for caring what she looked like at all and threw the red one back on just to be ornery.

She flounced down the staircase, holding her head high and bracing herself for her first glimpse of Ian. The great room and kitchen were empty. She passed them and headed down the hallway that led to a maze of other rooms, including a game room and a home theater, as well as rooms whose purposes she couldn't quite discern. At the very end was Ian's office. But the door was closed. Afraid that he might be in the middle of working on the case, she went back to the kitchen.

Her stomach chose that moment to rumble, reminding her that she'd eaten only one of her pieces of pizza last night after going most of the day without eating. She felt as if her stomach was going to rub right through her spine if she didn't have something soon.

The groceries in the refrigerator were probably a chef's dream. She imagined someone who knew how to cook really well could whip up an amazing omelet or some other kind of eggs and bacon, and maybe French toast. Since her breakfast cooking skills consisted of knowing how to pour a bowl of cereal or make toast, she did both—first the toast, then the cereal. She knew that much at least. No one liked soggy cereal.

After placing her dirty dishes in one of two drawer-style dishwashers, she thumped her hands on top of the island, wondering what to do next. Had Ian already eaten? Should she bring him some toast and cereal in his office? Rather than guess, she decided to brave the lion's den and simply ask him. She headed down the hallway toward his office.

"Morning. Looking for me?"

She turned around. Ian was coming down the stairs, looking so good in his jeans and black collared shirt that she had to remind herself to breathe. She also had to remind herself that he didn't want her in his life, even though he supposedly loved her. If she went down that rabbit hole again of trying to understand his reasoning, she'd just get herself twisted into knots. Instead, she forced a smile and tried to pretend that everything was normal, that he'd never told her he loved her.

And that she hadn't sat up most of the night trying to figure out whether she loved him too.

Not that it mattered. Love wasn't something she'd ever had in her life, and had never expected to have. How was she supposed to even recognize it? And since he hadn't asked her if she loved him back, did it even matter?

"Did you eat?" he asked as he headed into the kitchen.

"Cereal and toast. Want me to fix you some?"

He wrinkled his nose. "Not my idea of a good way to start the morning, but thanks just the same. I'll whip up an omelet."

Her mouth watered.

He glanced at her as if he could read her mind. "I'll make two, just in case you saved any room."

"I should politely say no since I already ate. But an omelet sounds wonderful."

"Bacon, cheese, peppers and tomatoes okay?"

"Better than okay. Perfect."

He smiled, but she noticed it didn't quite reach his eyes. Regret sat like a cold knot in her stomach.

They ate in strained silence, with an occasional polite inquiry or answer. She'd never felt uncomfortable around him before, and she longed for the easy friendship they'd shared for so many months.

After helping him clean up, she stood on the opposite side of the marble island. "What's the plan today? Are you going into town again to talk to more confidential informants?"

"I don't think so. I put the word out yesterday with the ones I spoke to about letting others know what kind of information I was seeking. One of them will call me if something comes up." He rubbed the back of his neck. "Honestly, I'm kind of at a loss, not knowing who to trust anymore."

"I don't understand. Did something else happen? Why don't you know who to trust?"

He studied her a long moment, then rounded the island. "Come to my office. I'll show you something."

She followed him down the long hall and stopped in surprise just inside what he'd referred to as his office. "This is a library, not an office."

He'd continued to the large desk sitting in the middle of the room and turned to look at her. Then he glanced around as if for the first time. "I suppose you could call it that. I hired someone to decorate this place. I don't really pay all that much attention to the details since I'm so rarely here."

She stopped beside one of the built-in bookshelves that lined every wall, for two full stories. A balcony that ran the perimeter of the room provided access to the higher shelves. Rolling ladders gave access to the lower ones. "I could read a book every day and never read all of these. This must be what heaven is like."

He shrugged and turned back to his desk.

Her delight in the space dampened with his lack of enthusiasm. She took a seat on the other side of his desk and waited to see what he wanted to show her.

He opened a laptop and typed for a moment, then turned it around, showing a picture of a yellow index card. "This was found in the warehouse where I was supposed to meet Butch and exchange money for Maria and the others."

"Okay." She crossed her arms on the desk so she could lean closer to read it. "Wait. I thought you said he didn't show, that your cover was blown. That card says to meet Wolverine in a parking lot for further instructions."

"It does. But it also says to smile for the camera. The warehouse was wired all over with cameras inside and out. And the original deal was no law enforcement or there was no deal. You were there. You saw what happened."

She nodded. "Within moments of you going inside the warehouse, cops and special agents poured out of the woods and went inside too. I thought that was planned, part of the sting to rescue the women."

"Yes, and to give them the benefit of the doubt, they did wait quite a while. Butch was a no-show. But I wanted to go inside and scope it out before they followed. Unfortunately, they didn't wait. And as a result, no deal. Butch disappeared."

"Did Wolverine show up the next day at the parking lot?"

He shook his head. "I was off the case officially then. But my contacts tell me that my boss staked out the lot all day, just in case Wolverine showed. He didn't."

She sat back. "Then he really is gone. The women have been taken somewhere else. I've lost my chance to rescue Maria."

"I'm not so sure. Homeland Security put a net around Gatlinburg before we even went to the warehouse. They've been working with the state, using agricultural inspections as a guise to search trucks traveling on the highways. Bus stations and airports are under heavy surveillance. There's no easy way for Butch to transport all those girls without coming under some kind of scrutiny. I imagine he's hunkered down somewhere, in a house, maybe a remote barn or something like that until the heat dies down."

The hope that had started to die inside her sputtered back to life. "That's good, if all those people are trying to find them. Someone will see something, notice something. There's still a chance. Right?"

"Yes and no. There are enough people involved so that Gatlinburg PD and Homeland Security have to make it look like they're working hard to prevent Butch from leaving with his victims. But I believe that someone on the inside, maybe even someone in the district attorney's office, is helping Butch, tipping him off so he can stay ahead of any searches. With them protecting him, it makes finding him nearly impossible."

He stared at her, his jaw tight. "In spite of me trying to convince you that most of us in law enforcement are the good guys, it appears that you may have been right to fear me and the people I work with." He punched a key on the laptop and another picture of a yellow index card appeared. "That's what was on the back of the index card in the warehouse."

For Homeland Security Agent Ian McKenzie.

She pressed a hand to her throat, immediately understanding. "Butch knew who you really were even before you went inside the warehouse, before the others showed up."

"He did. And only a handful of people knew my true identity. I've been deep undercover for a long time, putting everything into motion. The only way for him to have known I'm a special agent with Homeland Security is if one of the men I've trusted all this time betrayed me." He snapped the laptop shut and sat back. "That's what I meant earlier when I said I wasn't sure who to trust."

She swallowed, hard, and asked the question that she had to ask. "I knew who you really were. At least, I did in the days before the warehouse meeting. Am I on your list of suspects?"

He frowned, then blinked as if the idea had never occurred to him. He immediately shook his head. "Of course not. Even if you weren't vested in wanting your friend Maria rescued, you're not the kind of person who would do that."

She gave him a relieved smile. "I'm glad you know that I would never do something like that." She frowned. "Wait. If you found that index card in the warehouse, then whoever betrayed you knows that you know, right?"

"Not yet, or at least I don't think so. I was the only one there with the crime scene tech when he picked up the index card and turned it over. I haven't told anyone about what was on the back because I've been trying to dig into who's working the case to figure out who'd have a motive to help Butch. It's not like a murder scene where we're trying to get DNA or anything like that. Processing the index card isn't uppermost on anyone's priorities. It was dusted for fingerprints and came away clean. As far as I know, it's now sitting in an evidence locker. Eventually, someone will see it, I'm sure. But there's really no reason at present. The focus right now is on locating Butch and his victims."

"How short is your list of suspects?"

He held up his fingers and used them to list the people most likely involved. "My boss at Homeland Security, the Gatlinburg police chief, an assistant district attorney who's been our liaison all along in this investigation, the special agent who's been my liaison with my boss while undercover—"

"Chris Parker? The guy you asked to watch me at the duplex?"

He nodded and lowered his hands. "And you, of course. But I would never consider you as a suspect. Of the four I mentioned, Chris is the least likely. I called in an anonymous tip about him possibly accepting bribes, which initiated an immediate internal review of his finances. He's been put on paid leave while the investigation continues. But my boss mentioned it offhandedly in a status call yesterday when I asked him how the search for Butch was going. From what Nash says,

Chris's bank records look squeaky clean, so they realize the tip is likely wrong."

"And he's a friend of yours?"

He winced. "Yeah, I know. Heck of a way to treat a friend. But lives are on the line here. I'll tell him later why I did it. The most it does is inconvenience him and give him a paid vacation for a while. I'm sure he'll understand."

"I appreciate you letting me in on these details about the investigation. But I'm puzzled about why you did it."

"No more secrets or lies. That was my vow to you yesterday. And I know how much Maria means to you. I wanted to lay it all out there so you'd know what's being done to find her."

"You're a good man, Ian."

His mouth tilted in an almost-smile. "For a cop, right?"

"You're a good man, period. Proof that there are good cops out there. I'm just sorry it took me so long to realize it."

His gaze captured hers for a long moment, as if he was searching for something. Then he picked up the manila folder sitting on one side of his desk and set it in the middle. "I need to get back to studying the case file, diving into the backgrounds on my pool of suspects and seeing if there's anything I can do to steer the investigation based on my findings." He waved toward the bookshelves. "You're welcome to look around, find something to occupy your time while you have to stay here. I know you love to read."

She glanced longingly at the bookshelves, but shook her head. "Maybe later. Ian, how long do you think Butch will keep the women in hiding before he gives up?"

"Gives up? I don't see him ever turning himself in."

"That's not what I mean." She splayed her hands on top of the desk and drew a shaky breath before voicing her deepest fear. "If he feels the net around the city is too tight and he won't be able to escape with the women, do you think he'd try to escape on his own? Would he leave the women behind somewhere, locked up so they can't get away and tell anyone about him? Could they even now be without food, water, left on their own to…" She choked on the last word, but from the grave look in his gaze, she knew she didn't have to say it. And her questions didn't seem to surprise him either.

"You've already thought about that possibility, haven't you?"

He gave her a crisp nod. "It's my deepest fear, that we'll find them after it's too late to save them. Which is why I need to get back to work."

She put her hand on top of his, stopping him from opening the folder. "You need a sounding board, don't you? Someone other than me. Someone who's smart *and* has a background in law enforcement. Someone who knows the system and has established contacts over several decades. Someone who isn't currently connected with the police, Homeland Security or the district attorney's office, but yet knows the inner workings—I would imagine—of all three groups."

His jaw tightened, and he tugged his hand from beneath hers. "Don't, Shannon. Don't ask me to do that. You know I can't. You know why."

She gave him a sad smile. "Yes, I know why. Maybe it's time he knows why too. And maybe you can give him this chance to atone for what he did, and in the process save the lives of thirty women. Ian, the time has finally come. You need to go see your father."

He shoved back from his desk and left the room, firmly shutting the door behind him.

Shannon's shoulders slumped. In the span of just a few days, she'd managed to destroy her most treasured friendship. And now she'd made the man who'd professed to love her become the man who hated her. He'd trusted her enough to tell her about what happened all those years ago. He'd trusted her enough to tell her how he felt about her. And he'd trusted her enough to share details about the case, even though she knew it was against the rules of his job. And what had she done? She'd turned on him. Or at least that was how he must feel. And now he'd literally walked out of her life. There was no coming back from this. She'd well and truly lost him.

The door opened behind her. She turned in her chair to see Ian standing there in his black leather coat, carrying her jacket across his arm.

She stood and slowly crossed the room. "This is it, then, I guess. You're turning me over to someone else to guard me until the danger has passed?"

"No. We're going to see the Mighty McKenzie."

Chapter Twenty-One

When Ian pulled into the long row of paved parking spots in front of his parents' two-story cabin that rivaled his monstrosity in size, he didn't recognize any of the vehicles parked out front. But the green-and-white SUV with a National Park Service shield on the door was a big clue.

"Ian?" Shannon asked beside him. "Is something wrong?"

He arched a brow.

Her face flushed. "I mean, besides the fact that we're even here—which I sincerely appreciate. I know how hard it was to—"

He covered her hand with his. "It's okay, Shannon. I can never stay angry at you for long, and I'm way past that. It's just that asking my father for help in any way is a bitter pill to swallow." He motioned toward the other vehicles. "Especially since he took my phone call as an opportunity to stage a mini family reunion, or maybe an intervention. My brothers are here."

"Oh." She gave him an apologetic look. "I'm really, *really* sorry."

"If the Mighty McKenzie patriarch can help us rescue some victims of human trafficking, it will all be worth it." At least, that was what he kept telling himself.

One of the thick wooden double front doors opened and his mother stood there, smiling and waving. He could see the sparkle of tears on her cheeks. "Ah, hell. She's crying."

Shannon followed his gaze. "Your mom?"

"Margaret McKenzie, in the flesh." He squeezed her hand again. "Prepare yourself. She's a hugger."

The look of panic that swept over her face had him regretting his warning. "It's okay. If you want, I can be the bad guy and tell her to leave you alone, not to touch you. I'm pretty used to the bad-guy role in my family. I don't mind."

"No, no." She wiped her hands on her jeans and smiled through the windshield at his mother, who looked about ready to jump out of her skin waiting for them. "It's just…weird. I don't think my mother ever hugged me."

Ian was so stunned that he didn't get out of the Charger fast enough to open Shannon's door. Like the amazing woman she was, she marched right up to his mom and let herself be wrapped in what was likely a bone-crushing grip. His mom was almost as tall as him, and not exactly on the small side.

"Mom, let her go. I don't think she can breathe," he teased as he reached them.

"Oh, goodness. I'm so sorry." She smiled through her tears at Shannon. "It's just that Ian has never brought anyone home to meet us before." His mother held both of Shannon's hands in hers. "It *is* Shannon, right? I think that's what William said."

"Yes, ma'am."

Shannon seemed about ready to hyperventilate as she looked at Ian. He was about to correct his mother's assumption that they were a couple, but she didn't give him a chance. It was his turn for a bone-crushing hug.

A few moments later, a cough sounded behind her and she let him go, wiping her eyes. "It's been so long. I wish you'd visit more often."

"Let them in, Margaret. It's downright cold outside."

Ian stiffened at the sound of his father's voice. It was Shannon's turn to comfort him. She slid her hand in his and squeezed, then continued to hold his hand, which gave him the perfect excuse not to shake his father's hand as they moved into the foyer. Instead, he nodded.

His father nodded just as stiffly, then smiled warmly at Shannon. "Miss Murphy. I'm Ian's father, William. The woman who was crying all over you is his mom, Margaret. Welcome to our home."

"Um, thank you, sir. We, ah, appreciate your help, especially on such short notice."

Ian knew how intimidating his parents could be. Given Shannon's past and how uncomfortable she had to be meeting a former judge and prosecutor, he couldn't be prouder of her. He squeezed her hand again and smiled when she looked at him. She offered him a tentative smile in return.

His father's smile faded as he turned to Ian. "You indicated in our phone call that you're in a hurry, that the reason for this meeting is of an urgent nature. We can talk in my office." He smiled at Shannon again. "Miss Murphy, would you like to join us or would you prefer to stay out here with Margaret? I'm sure she'd love another opinion on the decorations she's planning for our sons' upcoming weddings here on the property."

Ian's mom surprised him by shaking her

head. "I can tell that Shannon wants to be a part of your discussion."

Shannon looked grateful when she met his mom's gaze. "Yes, ma'am. I'd like that very much."

Margaret smiled. "No problem, dear. You go on ahead with the men. Normally I'd insist on being a part of the discussion too. But I really am behind on helping make some decisions on the upcoming weddings. I'll get back to it." She headed toward the kitchen.

His father hesitated. "Might as well be comfortable. We'll meet in the great room instead of the office."

As if on cue, or as if they'd been listening, which was what Ian assumed, his brothers emerged from the hallway that led to the office. Shannon seemed to sink against his side as he reintroduced his brothers to her. He knew she was remembering their first meeting in the hospital, when they'd all pointed guns at her. To be fair, she'd aimed a gun at them too.

Ian chose a love seat to the left of the fireplace for him and Shannon. Once everyone was settled, he dove right in and brought them up to speed on what was happening with the human trafficking investigation and the dilemma he found himself in.

"I don't know who to trust. Someone on the inside had to have blown my cover. I can't think of any other way for them to have found out." To his family's credit, not one of them looked at Shannon with any suspicion or questioned whether she could be the mole.

Ian continued. "I can't even tell my boss about what was written on the other side of that index card without knowing whether he's the one who betrayed me. I'm at an impasse, and time is running out for the victims."

Adam sat forward. "Your boss put you on administrative leave. I'm putting my money on him being the mole."

"That's my thought too," Ian agreed. "He's never done anything before to make me suspect that I couldn't trust him. And I can't think of any reason for him to have suddenly turned to the dark side. But if he is sabotaging the search, then it's my duty to prove it so I can ensure that we have the best chance at actually finding and saving these young women." He grimaced. "And kids. From the pictures I saw, two of them are little more than children."

His father rested his forearms on his knees, looking deep in thought. "Either the chief of police is rotten, the special agent in charge at Homeland Security is rotten, or it's the assistant district attorney. Have I got that right? No one else knew about your cover?"

"I did," Shannon admitted. "Not all along, just recently. But I knew before the botched deal at the warehouse."

His father smiled kindly. "I appreciate that, Miss Murphy. But Ian is here with you, which means he trusts you one hundred percent. That's good enough for me."

She exchanged a surprised glance with Ian.

He gave his father a curt nod. "Thank you, sir." He cleared his throat. "There's one other person who knew—Special Agent Chris Parker. He's been my liaison in the field the whole time I've been here. Chris and I have been in the trenches together many times, and I don't feel that he could be involved. However, to be certain, I sent an anonymous tip to internal investigations that he was accepting bribes. They suspended him pending an investigation."

Duncan let out a bark of laughter. "I'll bet he loved and appreciated that."

"I'll make it up to him sometime. The investigation is ongoing. But they dove in fast, and everything is checking out. He's not our guy. That kind of strategy, an anonymous tip, won't fly for someone more senior like my boss. They'd investigate, but they'd be a lot more careful and would take their time. He wouldn't be suspended until they found credible evidence."

"You don't need to get him suspended," his dad offered. "You need to trick him, and the others. Keep it simple. The goal isn't to gather evidence for prosecution at this point. You need to identify the mole, remove him from the investigation so you can get the ball rolling and make sure every effort is truly being made to find the women. And those poor kids." He shook his head. "You won't need anything elaborate. Just fast."

"What do you suggest?" Ian asked.

"Pick three different locations for a sting operation. You can put out the word to each of your suspects that one of Butch's men contacted you and is willing to trade information and testify against everyone else involved if he can cut a deal. I'm assuming this Butch guy has enough men in his chain of command that it will fly."

Duncan nodded. "I like that. It's simple, like Dad said. And it lets you find out right away which one is your mole."

Shannon glanced around, then looked at Ian. "Everyone else looks like they understand. But I'm lost. How exactly will you find out who blew your cover?"

"My father is suggesting that I feed the same fake information to the police chief, my boss and the ADA and let them know that I'm meeting Butch's guy who's squealing on him. I tell them each a different location, but the same time. I'd have to get each of them to agree not to come there, that it has to be just me and the informant or they'll bolt. I can use the disastrous warehouse debacle as justification for going it alone. Whichever one of them shows up is the mole."

Shannon's eyes widened with alarm. "But won't the mole show up planning to try to kill you and the informant?"

"Yes, but I wouldn't give him that opportunity. I'd pick locations with limited access, then spy on all the approaches using long-range binoculars. It won't matter if he tries to ambush me. I won't be in a position for him to get me. The goal is just to find out who shows up. Low risk, high reward." He nodded. "It could work." He stood, and this time he offered his father his hand. "Thank you, sir. Sometimes an obvious answer is hard to see when you're deep inside of the problem you're trying to solve. I appreciate your perspective."

Everyone stood.

His father smiled as he shook Ian's hand. "Happy to help, son."

"You can't be in three places at once," Adam said. "And you're still pursuing the investigation on the side, isn't that right?"

Ian shrugged. "I've got a few contacts I can tap, see if they'll help." He put his hand on Shannon's back to lead her out.

"You already have three people right here who can help." This time it was Duncan who spoke.

Ian stared at him in surprise. "Are you volunteering?"

His three brothers exchanged looks, then nodded in unison.

"We all are," Colin said.

"Why?" Ian asked. "Why would you offer to do that?"

Adam stepped forward and put his hand on Ian's good shoulder, probably remembering that his left one was still sore. "We're family. That's what family does. We have each other's backs. Let us do this for you."

Ian studied each of them, automatically suspicious of their motives. "What do you get in return? What do you want?"

Shannon gasped beside him. "Ian, I think they really do want to help."

Colin grinned. "He's right, lass. There's a catch."

"I knew it," Ian grumbled.

Duncan and Adam frowned as if they had no idea what their brother was talking about.

"Just a minute." Colin jogged to a decorative table against the far wall that was stacked with envelopes. He brought one back and handed it to Ian. "Your official wedding invitation. Agree to be there, and we'll help you find your mole. Using us will be way faster than you having to find three other people in a short time frame like this."

Ian reluctantly took the envelope. "This is blackmail. I'm pretty sure you're committing a felony right now."

Colin's grin widened. "Peyton will be thrilled to see you there."

Duncan smiled. "Remi has been dying of curiosity to meet you. She'll be happy to see you there too. Thanks, Ian."

He gave them a curt nod, still not comfortable with the way they were all getting along these days. Maybe he should start a fistfight just to get his world back on its normal axis.

An hour later they'd planned out the locations, time, and Ian had finished contacting the ADA, police chief and his boss to set everything up. He rose again to leave. But when he held out his hand to Shannon, she shook her head and settled back against the love seat.

"I'm not going anywhere," she insisted, crossing her arms.

Ian sat back down and leaned in close so he could whisper. "Are you okay? What's wrong?"

She gave him an irritated look and made no attempt to whisper her reply. "Your brothers don't have to leave right away since the meeting time everyone agreed to is several hours from now. Which means we all have time to address the elephant in the room. Ian, I think it's high time that you told your father why you ran off when you were eighteen. It's time for you to tell him why you've resented him all these years. You need to tell him about Willow."

Ian's entire body flushed hot and cold as he stared at the one person he'd trusted, ever, with his secret. And now she was throwing it out in front of his family like a bone to a dog.

"Why are you doing this to me?" he whispered harshly.

"Willow?" his father asked behind him. "Is she talking about Willow Rivera?"

Ian ignored him and continued to look at Shannon. "Why?"

"Because I know what it's like to harbor resentments inside you. You nurture your wounds and feed them until they fester like poison. You have to get them out in order to heal. You have to forgive in order to move on and find peace."

"What do you know about getting out the poison and moving on?" he bit out.

She stiffened but didn't look away. "I forgive you for lying to me."

He stared at her in shock. "You forgive me?"

"Who's Willow Rivera?" Colin asked.

"Beats me," Adam replied.

Shannon took Ian's hands in hers, her eyes brimming with tears. "I do. I forgive you. And I trust you, with all my heart. I really do. And that's what I want for you. I want you to get the poison out and begin to heal."

"Ian?" His father sounded shaken. "Please, son. What's this about?"

Uncaring of his audience, Ian cupped Shannon's beloved face in his hands and kissed her. When he pulled back, she shuddered and gave him a fierce hug. He held her a long moment, then kissed her again before sitting back beside her with his arm around her shoulders. But this time he wasn't trying to give her strength. He was drawing his strength from her.

His brothers and father stared at him, a host of confused expressions on their faces as they each sat back down and waited.

Ian announced to the room at large, "Willow Rivera was an eighteen-year-old woman I met when I was fifteen. Father found out about her and thought she was a bad influence on me. He ordered me not to see her anymore. I tried to explain to him about our relationship and what was really going on. I tried many times. But he refused to listen."

His father's face reddened. "There was nothing to explain. She had a criminal record, for prostitution. What has this got to do with anything?"

"You refused to listen," Ian repeated. "Willow needed help, not condemnation. She wasn't a prostitute by choice. She was a victim. Her stepfather was pimping her out, beating her, withholding food. He forced her to walk the streets. I was her friend. I was trying to help her. But when she needed me the most, you essentially kidnapped me and took me up to a cabin hundreds of miles away for a two-week father-son fishing trip. You tricked me into going with you. Had I known we'd be gone that long, I would have refused to go."

His father frowned. "I was trying to get my son away from a bad influence."

Ian gritted his teeth. "When we finally came back," Ian said, "Willow was gone."

"Thank God," his father said.

Ian stared at him incredulously. "God had nothing to do with her fate. You can chalk that up to the Mighty McKenzie. She was desperate, with nowhere to turn. Her one friend in the whole world—" he thumped his chest "—me, I wasn't there for her. She ran away to escape her abusive stepfather and got taken in by what we now call a human trafficker. He killed her, Dad. You failed her. We both failed her. And she paid for our sins with her life."

His father's face turned ghost-white. "That's why you hate me? You blame me for her death?"

Ian closed his eyes for a long moment, then slowly shook his head and met his father's tortured gaze. "I don't hate you. I thought I did, for a very long time. But I hated myself even more, for not standing up to you, for being too afraid to outshout Mighty McKenzie and make him listen. Every time I tried to tell you the truth about her, you shut me down. I should have fought harder, made you listen. After her death, I was so disgusted and ashamed that I became the juvenile delin-quent you believed me to be. And from then on out, everything I did was to spite you. If I was doing too well in school, I'd purposely not turn in an assignment or flunk a test. You wanted me to go to college, so I ran off the day I turned eighteen, determined that you would never see me make anything of my life. I wanted you to feel like a failure because I'd failed already, in the worst possible way, and blamed you."

His father's eyes were bright with unshed tears. He cleared his throat. "But you're with Homeland Security. I don't—"

"Understand how they'd take a total screwup?" Ian glanced at his brothers, who were riveted on the conversation but, surpris-ingly, weren't jumping in to tell him what an idiot he was. Beside him, Shannon had tucked herself against him and had her hand on his back, as if to give him strength. The anger that had been flowing through him as he re-counted his disastrous youth seemed to drain away. "I went to college on a full scholarship. I just never told you about it. I got a degree in criminal justice and worked briefly as a sheriff's office intern before joining Home-land Security. I became what you wanted me to be. But I never told you, because I didn't want you to have that satisfaction. And I've spent my entire life blaming you every time something went wrong, when all along—" he blew out a deep breath "—it was my failings that haunted me."

His father tentatively put his hand on Ian's shoulder and stared deep into his eyes. "I was so worried about you, thinking that woman—"

"Willow."

He swallowed. "Willow. I thought I was protecting my son. I cut off every conversation where you tried to bring her up, because I was so upset that I'd failed you in the first place by not realizing you were associating with someone whom I thought to be a bad influence, until it was nearly too late. I thought I was doing the right thing." He shook his head. "I was wrong. I'm so sorry, son. So deeply sorry that I hurt you, and that Willow paid the price for my stubbornness."

"I'm sorry too." This time it was Adam who spoke. "I was your big brother. When you started to rebel and get in trouble, I should have sat you down and talked it out, found out what was really going on. Instead, I let my anger drive my actions. I should have been there for you, but I wasn't. I'm sorry, Ian."

Duncan cleared his throat, looking decidedly uncomfortable. "We were all too quick to judge you. We were your worst tormentors as teenagers. We should have had your back. Instead, we just got mad because it seemed like you were getting all of the attention, bringing the family down, making Mom and Dad look bad to their friends. We should have known there was a reason you were acting out. But none of us took the time to ask you. I wish I could have a do-over, Ian. But hopefully we can move forward and have a new start. That's the best I can offer. But it's a sincere offer. I want you in my life, in our lives."

His father, who still had his hand on Ian's shoulder, nodded in agreement, as did Adam.

Colin slapped his hands on top of his thighs and looked around at all of them. "I agree that Adam and Duncan were total jerks growing up. It's about time they apologized for it."

Adam and Duncan both shoved him off the couch onto the floor.

"Hey, hey, quit picking on the favorite son here." Colin grinned, then pointed at Ian. "Made you smile."

Ian shook his head, surprised to realize that he was indeed smiling at his brothers' antics.

His father's hand tightened on his shoulder. "I love you, son. More than you'll ever know.

I hope you'll give me the opportunity to prove it, and be a part of our lives going forward. I don't deserve it. But I'm asking you to give me a chance." He stood and held out his hand.

Ian hesitated. He'd never expected this moment to come in his life. His father had been the villain of his story for so long. Even as an adult when he'd finally realized he'd overblown his father's culpability, that he was using him as a crutch, blaming everything wrong in his life on his relationship with his father, he'd never once envisioned a moment where they'd be able to set the hurts of the past aside. And if it wasn't for Shannon, he'd never have known how badly he wanted to do that.

He stood and shook his father's hand.

His mother came into the room, wiping her hands on her apron and smiling. "I've got fresh-baked chocolate-chip cookies and some…" She blinked and stared at Ian and his dad, who still hadn't let go of Ian's hand. "Ian? William?" She couldn't seem to formulate anything beyond that.

Colin jumped up from the floor and shoved Adam and Duncan before hurrying out of their reach to stand beside his mother. "Cookies sound great, Ma. I'm starving." He put his arm around her shoulders and pulled her with him toward the kitchen.

Adam and Duncan got up, shaking their heads.

"You're always starving," Adam accused.

Shannon smiled up at Ian from the couch.

His father let his hand go and motioned toward the kitchen. "Your mother still makes the best chocolate-chip cookies in Tennessee. And she won't let you leave without trying them. You might as well give in." He winked at Shannon, then followed the others out of the room.

Ian pulled Shannon to her feet and wrapped his arms around her, holding her tight. "I was furious with you for starting all of that. Now I realize you're wise beyond your years. I feel like a weight has lifted off my shoulders. Maybe not quite all the way yet, but mostly."

"It will take more than one conversation and a handshake to heal your soul, Ian. It took me years to forgive my mom for what she did to me. But when I did, I realized forgiveness is something you do for yourself, not for others. It's important to forgive in order to move on. I'm so glad you're beginning to feel that same joy."

He stared at her in wonder. "About what I said, at the cabin. I'm not so sure that I—"

"Ian, Shannon." Colin stood on the other side of the room. "You coming or what? Adam's scarfing down all the cookies. We'll have to roll him out the door later."

"I heard that," Adam yelled from the kitchen.

Colin grinned and winked before disappearing again.

Ian took Shannon's hand. "Come on. It looks like the rule is that when you more or less reconcile with your family, you have to eat chocolate-chip cookies."

"I can think of worse things."

They headed into the kitchen.

A short time later, Ian led Shannon outside to his car. He held the passenger door open for her, then pulled her in for a kiss. When he finally came up for air, she pressed a shaking hand against his chest.

"Wow," she breathed. "Whatever I did to deserve that, let me know so I can do it again."

He grinned, feeling lighter than he had in a long time. But as they headed back down the mountain, the reality of what still remained to be done and the life-and-death stakes pressed in on him. "After I drop you off at my cabin, I'm going to check in on my confidential informants and look around town to see if there have been any sightings of Butch or the others. Eventually I'll head to the duplex and get us both some fresh clothes. Even with my brothers' help, I don't know how many more days this thing will drag on."

"I'm sure I can amuse myself with that wall of electronics at your cabin, or that library. It makes me drool just thinking about all of those books. Although if you don't mind grabbing the book I was reading at my house, that would be great. I'd like to finish it."

"The Lisa Gardner thriller?"

She blinked. "You remember which book I was reading? I'm impressed."

"Yeah, well. I'm a special agent, you know. I notice things like that."

She rolled her eyes.

He grinned.

When he pulled into the driveway, he started to get out, but she put her hand on his. "You've given me your alarm code, a door key and the phone number for your current burner phone. I think I can handle walking myself to the front door. Go on. You have a lot to do. I'll be fine."

He cupped her face and kissed her, but forced himself not to deepen the kiss, or he'd be there all day. He wanted her so much. And there were things he needed to tell her, things that had surprised him, things he'd never expected until he'd sat in the kitchen with his family today and looked around and, for the first time, felt like maybe he just might belong. But those things, those epiphanies about himself—about the future he now realized he wanted—would have to wait.

After watching to make sure that she got in okay, he took off down the winding mountain road toward Gatlinburg.

Chapter Twenty-Two

Shannon had just finished straightening up the kitchen after lunch when the doorbell rang. She froze, not sure what to do. No one knew that Ian McKenzie lived here, not even his family.

If he'd ordered a package to be delivered, he'd have told her. She was sure of it.

Her gun was upstairs, in the bedside table. Should she get it? Or just ignore whoever was at the door and hope they'd go away?

The doorbell rang again. She jogged to the stairs to get her gun. Then she'd call Ian and—

"Shannon?" a woman's muffled voice called through the front door.

She froze, her hand tightening on the railing. This wasn't possible. It had to be a trick. That voice couldn't be who it sounded like.

A frantic knock echoed in the foyer. "Shannon, it's Maria. Please. I came to warn you. They're on their way here."

The palpable fear in the woman's voice along with her words sent a chill snaking up Shannon's spine.

"Please, hurry. Shannon?" The doorbell rang several more times. "Hurry! If they see me standing out here, warning you, they'll kill me. Let me in."

Shannon ran to the front door and looked through the peephole. A sob caught in her throat when she saw that her ears weren't playing tricks on her. Maria stood there in a tattered blue dress and bare feet, dark curly hair matted and whipping around her face in the frigid wintry air. She didn't have a coat. Her entire body shook, either from the cold or fear, probably both. Her dark brown eyes looked hollow and bleak. Tears streamed down her face.

Behind her in the driveway was a bright yellow Camaro with the driver's door standing open. It was parked sideways as if Maria had turned a half circle for a quick getaway. With the house's elevated position in front of the steep driveway, Shannon could clearly see that no one else was in the car. She looked left and right. The road that wound around the mountain out front was clear.

"Shannon, please—"

"Maria," she called through the door, desperately wanting to open it. But none of this made sense. "What's going on? How did you know I was here?"

"I heard them talking about you, the men holding me. One of them said they found out your boyfriend was a special agent, and discovered where his parents lived. They hid in the woods by the parents' cabin. You were there with the agent earlier today, right?"

Shannon pressed a hand to her throat. "How did you know that?"

"I told you. I heard them. They put a GPS tracker on your boyfriend's car and got this address. They're planning an ambush. Let me in before they get here or we're both dead. Please!"

An ambush? Oh, no. She had to warn Ian.

"Come on," Maria pleaded, looking over her shoulder. She banged on the door again.

Shannon threw it open and wrapped her arms around her friend. Maria clung to her, tears wetting Shannon's blouse.

"I can't believe you're actually here," Shannon said. "I'd almost given up hope of finding you. Don't worry. I'll call Ian and he'll—" Behind her a rapid beep started in the hall.

Maria shoved out of her arms. "I think that's your alarm. It's about to go off."

"Oh. Hang on." She ran to the keypad and entered the code, disabling the security system.

"I'm so sorry, Shannon. He was going to kill my baby. I didn't have a choice."

Shannon turned, her mouth dropping open in shock. Maria was now clutching an infant against her chest, wrapped in a yellow blanket.

Beside her was the tall, lanky man who must have handed her the child. Shannon recognized him as one of the men she'd seen at the truck stop when Ian had told her to wait in the car.

Ian had called him Wolverine.

Greasy hair hung to his shoulders. A triumphant grin curved his lips as he aimed a pistol at her.

She slowly raised her hands. "What do you want?"

He cocked his head, as if contemplating her question. "What do I want? Hmm. I want a lot of things. I want to make a living without interference from do-gooders. I want the money I would have made from this latest shipment. But mostly, I want to kill a very special agent, the one who ruined everything and brought the heat down on our operation. And after I saw that tender kiss he gave you outside his family's cabin, I decided a bullet was too good for him. It will be much more enjoyable to make him suffer, by making you suffer." He narrowed his eyes and stepped closer. "Then I'll kill you both." He slammed the side of the pistol against her head.

Chapter Twenty-Three

With still no sightings of Butch or his minions, Ian finally headed to the duplex. Once he had another duffel loaded with shoes and clothes for both him and Shannon, he started for the garage. He'd only made it to the couch before his phone rang. It was Adam. He plopped the duffel onto the couch beside him and sat to take the call.

"The ADA was a no-show," Adam announced. "Which is good to know. Cameron Ellison always seemed like a stand-up guy to me. I'd worked with him in Memphis before both of us moved back here. I'm glad I didn't completely misjudge him."

"You know Ellison personally? From your Memphis days?"

"Personally might be stretching it. But professionally, yeah. He always seemed fair, and had a great prosecution record. Looks like you can mark him off the list of potential suspects for blowing your cover."

"That's good to know. Thanks. Really appreciate your help."

A few minutes later, Duncan checked in, followed by Colin. They both said pretty much the same thing as Adam. Neither the police chief nor Ian's boss at Homeland Security took the bait. After thanking them, Ian called his boss to tell him everything that he'd been doing. He told him about Wolverine being Andrew Branum, about his lack of success in any of his informants seeing or hearing any word on the street about any of the traffickers they were trying to find. Lastly, he told him about the evidence on the back of the index card. He had to hold the phone away from his ear while his boss yelled obscenities at him for even suspecting he could be a mole. It took several minutes to calm him down.

"Have you made any progress in the investigation?" Ian asked.

"Not much better than you. I've got the full cooperation of Gatlinburg PD as well as our guys, resources coming at me left and right. But we still don't have a lead on where the women are being held."

"Maybe knowing Wolverine's real name will help shake something loose on your end.

I had someone look him up but he didn't find any assets here in town. And I haven't figured out the real names of the other two thugs that work for Gillespie. So, basically, I've got nothing."

"I'll get some of my guys to dig deep into this Andrew Branum. Maybe he's hidden assets under some shell companies. Everything else has been a bust so far. The BOLO on his yellow Beetle hasn't yielded any sightings. If he's still in town, he's driving something else now."

"About my administrative leave—"

"Ah, hell. Consider it over. It's not like you really took a break anyway. Might as well be official so you can commandeer any resources you need in a pinch. But once this thing is over, you're taking some time off. A lot of it. That's an order."

Ian grinned as he ended the call and slid the phone into the pocket of his leather coat. He reached for the duffel, then paused. If the ADA, police chief and his boss weren't moles, then how had Butch and his men found out that he worked for Homeland Security? He couldn't think of anyone else who knew his secret, aside from Shannon, Chris and, of course, his brothers. None of those were viable possibilities. Who, then?

No one. There just wasn't anyone else.

Then how?

He sat on the couch, thinking it through, looking at every angle. He thought back to all the times when he'd even discussed the fact that his real name was Ian McKenzie, and that he was a special agent with Homeland Security. And he realized there just weren't that many times he'd said those two things out loud. Even in his dealings with his liaison, Chris, everything was in code. When they spoke, they made cryptic references to what they were doing, or put things in writing—which was rare—and then destroyed those messages immediately. Heck, the only place he'd ever spoken to Chris openly about their mission was when he'd brought him to the duplex to guard Shannon.

He straightened. It was also at the duplex where he'd spoken to her about being a special agent. He'd been in her bedroom and apologized for all the lies. And he'd been in jail all night right before that. If Wolverine saw him being arrested, which he'd assumed he would since the van had left right before the police arrived, then he would have known his side of the duplex would be empty.

His blood ran cold. He jumped up and started tossing the place, looking under lamps, taking apart the smoke detectors in the ceiling, unscrewing light switches. Then he stood at the kitchen counter looking down at the results of his search—six electronic listening devices, three from Shannon's side of the duplex and three from his. Knowing that the traffickers had been in Shannon's home had him sick to his stomach. Thank God she hadn't been hurt.

He stared at the transmitters. They were still on and sending data. Which meant that everything he'd just said to his boss had been heard by whoever was on the other end of the bugs.

He swore.

If his boss was right, and Wolverine did have assets in town hidden under a maze of shell companies, it wasn't likely that he'd be sitting around waiting for them if they showed up to seize those assets. Wolverine was in the wind now, on the run. So how were they going to find him?

Ian pondered that question as he smashed the devices. Then he grabbed the duffel and headed into the garage. He was about to get in his car when another thought occurred to him. If Butch's men had bugged the duplex after becoming suspicious that Ian was a cop, could they have done something else? Like put a tracker on his car?

He didn't see how. Since that night at the hospital, he'd kept his car in the garage specifically because of the fear that someone might put a tracker on it. He'd parked it on the street out front only once, hoping to draw Butch's men out. But he'd watched it the whole time. No one had come near it.

Plus, every time he'd come back to the duplex or driven around town, he'd taken the long way back to his cabin outside of Gatlinburg for the specific purpose of making sure that no one could follow him. In fact, the only time the Charger had been out of his sight was when he'd gone to the café to talk to Adam. But, as always, he'd kept an eye on his mirrors and drove a circuitous route to ensure that no one followed him to the café. There was no reason to think that anyone would have randomly seen his car parked behind the building and decided to put a tracker on it.

He shook his head. He was getting paranoid. He tossed the duffel into the back seat and slid behind the wheel when it occurred to him that there *was* one place he'd gone where he hadn't parked in a garage. A place where he'd been for several hours without being in view of his car.

His parents' cabin.

No one could have followed him there

without him knowing. But Butch and his men knew his real identity. A short internet search would lead them to the Mighty McKenzie, and his parents' cabin. They could have hidden in the woods, waiting to see whether he'd show up at the house. But when they saw the National Park Service SUV parked out front, they decided it was too risky to shoot him there. Instead, they could hide a GPS device on his car while he was inside, and attack him later when he wasn't with other law enforcement officers.

He shoved the door open and made a quick check of the car's underbelly. A few minutes later, he stared in growing dread at the magnetic tracking device that he'd found in the rear wheel well. They'd known every place he'd gone since leaving his parents' home. Which meant they knew where his cabin was located, and where he'd left Shannon, alone.

Oh, dear God. Please, no.

He grabbed his phone in a panic and pressed the button for his home number.

No one answered.

SHANNON WOKE TO the rancid smell of unwashed bodies and urine, and to the worst headache she'd ever had. She groaned and reached for her head.

"Don't," a familiar-sounding voice told her as fingers slid up Shannon's arm and gently eased her hand back down. "Don't move or even try to talk. And please don't touch your head. I just got it to stop bleeding. I don't want you bumping it and starting it up again."

"Maria?" Her voice sounded as groggy as she felt. "Is that you?" She blinked, but she couldn't see anything. It was pitch-dark. She blinked again, panic rising inside her. "I can't see."

"Shh, it's okay. None of us can. The cops are searching for them, so no lights. Nothing that might give away our location. It sucks, but it is what it is. There's a portable toilet in the corner. And some bottles of water and a small stash of food. You need to pee? I can help you to the toilet."

She started to shake her head, then realized Maria couldn't see her. "No. Where are we? What happened? You had a baby in your arms. And then that awful man—"

"Wolverine. That's what the little twerp likes to call himself. And it fits, in spite of how scrawny he looks. He's like a rabid animal and he'll turn on you in a second, tear you to pieces. Shannon, sweetie, I'm so sorry for betraying you. I didn't have a choice. He had my baby. He was going to kill her. He forced me to go up there and draw you out of the house. I didn't want—"

"Stop. I understand. I'm just glad that you're okay. But how did he know to use you to draw me out?"

"I've talked about you often enough that he knew we were friends. Once he figured out that you had a connection to that special agent—"

"Ian."

"Right. Once he heard that, he came up with a plan to use me as bait. I'm really sorry."

"It's all right. We're both alive. And so is your baby. That's what matters. But we need to get out of here if we're going to stay alive. We need to—"

A loud metallic screech was followed by a blast of sunlight. She raised her hand to shade her eyes, blinking to try to focus with the sudden change in light.

"No, leave us alone," Maria yelled. She cowered over a small yellow blanket, shielding her child with her body. And for the first time, Shannon realized where they were. And that she wasn't alone. There were dozens of women—most of them painfully young—huddled around each other like cattle in a barn.

A shadow fell over her. She looked up at a man, his features obscured because the sun was behind him. But she'd know that silhouette anywhere. He was the man who'd hit her back at Ian's house—Wolverine.

Two more men stood off to his right, one to his left. She recognized all of them from the truck stop meeting. Ian had been trying to locate Maria while rescuing human trafficking victims in his constant bid to atone for what had happened to Willow. Or at least that was what Shannon had thought. Now she knew he was also doing it as part of his job. Most likely the women he'd been trying to save were the same ones stuffed into this tight space with her right now.

Wolverine motioned toward the men on his right. "Hulk, Blade, put the fear of God into our girls. I don't want anyone making any noise and giving us away."

Our girls? Why was he talking like the boss, instead of one of the lackeys?

The red-haired man gave Wolverine an aggravated look. "You know I hate that nickname."

"Yeah, well. I like it. Go on."

Wolverine turned to the man on his left. "Grab her."

Shannon jerked back but he lifted her off the floor, pinning her arms to her sides. She drew breath to scream, but Wolverine slapped a piece of duct tape over her mouth.

Chapter Twenty-Four

Ian paced back and forth in front of the fireplace in his cabin, trying to blot out the sounds of the police and special agents on the phone, rattling papers and milling around in what had become their impromptu headquarters for the search for Shannon. He kept replaying the events of the past few days over and over in his mind. But he was coming up empty. He'd followed every possible lead to find Maria and the others. And now the traffickers had Shannon too. And much to Ian's surprise, he now knew that it was Wolverine who was their leader, not Butch. There was no question about that. Wolverine had jammed a knife into the log wall outside the front door, impaling a bright yellow index card that read, YOUR GIRLFRIEND DIES TONIGHT.

And just in case Ian hadn't finally connected the dots of yet another yellow index card to Wolverine's love of yellow clothes and cars, Wolverine had done him the favor of actually signing his name.

Ian reached the end of the room and turned around again. Nash rushed in from the kitchen area, where he'd been speaking to a group of agents studying the maps spread out on top of the island.

"What?" Ian demanded. "You've got something?"

Nash held his hands out. "We haven't found her yet. But I was right about the Andrew Branum name leading us through shell companies. He has a home in the Smokies just west of Gatlinburg. And he didn't get a chance to strip the place before we found it. The home is a treasure trove. Pictures, journals, cash." He handed his phone to Ian. "Recognize any of those guys? The team at the house took pictures of photographs inside Branum's home office. They seem to match your descriptions of the thugs that hang with him."

Ian swiped through the pictures. "Hulk, Blade, Jack. That's them." He handed the phone back.

"In addition to Butch Gillespie—your Hulk fellow—we've got the other two guys' real names now. Our buddies at the FBI ran their pictures from the Branum house search through their facial recognition database and got hits. We're following up on last-known addresses and getting warrants to search their properties. But Branum is the only local. The other guys are from out of state."

Ian grimaced. "Which means they're dead ends as far as leading to somewhere around here and finding Shannon."

"Maybe, maybe not. We've got their pictures now, and we're circulating them all over the place. Someone has to have seen them." He put his hand on Ian's shoulder. "I'll let you know when I've got something more." He motioned toward one of the groups of agents, and they headed down the hallway toward Ian's office.

"Nice place."

Ian turned to see Adam striding in from the foyer. Behind him were Duncan and Colin.

Stunned to see them, Ian asked, "What are you doing here?"

"Alerts about Shannon's abduction have been sent to everyone in law enforcement in a hundred-mile radius. A few quick calls and we heard the task force is forming right here, in my brother's cabin, which I didn't know about."

Ian rubbed the back of his neck, not sure what to say. "I don't... I should have—"

"I was teasing," Adam said. "I'm just not that good at it. Seriously, we're here to help. What's been done so far? What's the status of the search?"

Colin and Duncan flanked him, both nodding to indicate their willingness to help in the hunt for Shannon.

Ian brought them up to speed. "We've got people everywhere looking. Except for going door-to-door to every single cabin in the Smoky Mountains, I'm at a loss." He fisted his hands at his sides. "I've never felt so helpless in my life."

"What about the truck stop?" Adam asked. "Hiding Shannon and the other women in the back of one of those semis would be the perfect setup. Easily mobile, if it wasn't for all the roadblocks and traffic stops that are being done. He could have the women sitting there waiting until the cops give up. Then he just drives away."

"It's been searched already."

Colin and Duncan exchanged a surprised glance. Duncan said, "There must be two hundred semis parked there on any given day. Shannon's only been missing for a few hours."

"It was searched a few days ago while trying to find the thirty women that we believed Butch Gillespie was keeping prisoner. Of course, now it seems that Branum, Wolverine, is our main guy. Anyway, it wouldn't make sense for him to risk going in there for one person. He'd take Shannon wherever he's keeping the others, to consolidate resources."

"Every truck was searched?" Colin asked. "How did your boss get warrants to search every single truck?"

Ian frowned and glanced down the hall where Nash had disappeared. "I didn't ask him for the details. I was supposed to be on administrative leave at the time. I just assumed... Ah, hell." He strode down the hallway with his brothers following behind.

Nash was talking to some other agents working at Ian's desk. Without preamble, Ian interrupted him. "When you had the truck stop searched, did our guys go inside every truck?"

"I can answer that," one of the other agents said. "I was in charge of the search. Of the two hundred ten vehicles there at the time, the owners of one hundred seventy-two of them agreed to a search, which we did."

"And the remaining thirty-eight?" Ian demanded. "What about those?"

"Some left without being searched." He held his hands up. "We couldn't legally stop them on private property without a warrant, and we don't have probable cause to get warrants without some kind of evidence specific to each truck. But our nets around the city have been effective. Each semi is forced to stop at an agricultural inspection station out on the highway. We're using the regulations in place to force searches. It's been one hundred percent effective."

"Except that you haven't found the missing women yet," Adam added.

The agent's face flushed. "Not yet."

"How many of the original thirty-eight are still at the truck stop?" Ian asked. "Any of them?"

The agent swallowed and pulled out his phone. He thumbed through a series of texts, then said, "Ten. There are ten rigs we haven't searched that are still there."

Nash joined the conversation. "What are the odds of getting warrants to search them?"

"Pretty much zero, sir. No one has reported seeing anything unusual, nothing we can use to get a judge to sign a warrant."

"What about *smelling* something unusual?" Adam pulled out his phone. "You cram a bunch of people in a small, tight container like that, even during the winter it's going to stink. A cornucopia for air-scent tracking canines. If one of them alerts on a container, you've got your probable cause. No warrant needed."

He stepped away from them to speak on the phone for a moment. When he returned, he said, "I've got one of the National Park Service's search-and-rescue teams on their way to the truck stop right now. ETA is only five minutes. The dog handler lives down the road from the truck stop."

Nash motioned toward the agent who'd been in charge of the original search. "Get our guys in the area to head over to the truck stop. Have them meet the SAR team and show them which rigs to check out."

"On it." He punched some numbers on his phone.

Ian moved to stand beside his brothers, so tense he felt like he'd explode any second. About ten minutes later, Nash's phone rang. He answered, then set the phone on the desk. "You're on speaker, Special Agent Bledzinski. Give us the status."

"Yes, sir. The dog's here now. An agent is with the handler, directing him to the trucks."

The room went quiet, everyone listening as the agent continued to broadcast the status of the search.

"What's taking so long?" Nash demanded. "We're only talking ten trucks."

"Yes, sir, but it's a huge area to cover. The ones we need to search are spread out all over the place."

"Is there a yellow one?" Ian asked. "I remember a yellow rig at the back-left corner when I met Wolverine and his men there. He's got a weird fascination with the color yellow."

Nash nodded. "Did you hear that, Bledzinski?"

"Yes, sir. That rig is on our list. We'll head there right now."

Ian's stomach flipped. Adam put a hand on his shoulder while Colin and Duncan flanked him on the other side, all of them waiting.

An excited bark sounded through the phone.

"He's alerted on the trailer, sir!" Bledzinski yelled.

Ian waited, barely breathing as he listened intently.

"No driver. The back is padlocked. They're cutting it now."

Ian closed his eyes. Adam's hand tightened on his shoulder.

Chaos erupted through the phone. Some screams, shouts.

"Bledzinski," Nash demanded. "Sitrep. What's going on? Bledzinski?"

"Just a moment, sir." There was more noise in the background, then the sound of static before Bledzinski's voice sounded through the speaker again. "We've got them, sir. Thirty-one souls. And they're all alive."

A chorus of yells sounded behind them where other agents and police had come into the office to listen to the search in progress.

Adam grinned at Ian. "Thirty-one. You said there were thirty, plus Shannon makes thirty-one."

Ian forced a smile, but until he knew for sure that she'd been found, he wasn't ready to celebrate. He crossed to the desk. His boss was on the side of the room now, speaking to some of the policemen. His phone was still sitting on the desk. Ian picked it up and spoke into it. "Special Agent Bledzinski, can you confirm that one of the women is Shannon Murphy?"

"Of course. Hold on, sir." He could be heard in the background yelling over the noise, asking if one of the women was named Shannon Murphy.

It was an agonizing few minutes before he finally came back on the line. "Negative, sir. According to a woman here with a baby, Shannon was here. But she was taken away before we arrived."

Ian squeezed his eyes shut. Thirty-one, the thirty women in the photographs, plus a baby. Not Shannon.

"How long?" he asked, his voice hoarse. "How long ago was she taken away?"

"Approximately fifteen minutes, sir."

The room went silent again. Ian wanted to shout and storm and rage. Fifteen minutes. They'd missed her by fifteen minutes. But venting his anguish wouldn't help her. And every moment he stood here doing nothing was a minute more that she was in Wolverine's clutches.

He grabbed the phone and began barking orders as he ran toward the kitchen. "See if the witness saw the vehicle that took Shannon. Check the surveillance video. Find out which way it turned once it left the truck stop. Put out a BOLO and get officers out on I-40. I need a description of that car, Bledzinski."

"Yes, sir. Working on it."

Ian stopped in front of the kitchen island and shoved his way in between some of the agents to look at the large map spread out on top.

"Hey, wait a minute, here," the agent complained.

"Back off." Colin moved into the room, followed by Adam and Duncan. "Give him space."

"Do it." Nash ran in, slightly out of breath. He wedged his way in beside Ian. "We'll talk about chain of command later, McKenzie. But I've got your car description." He plopped a piece of paper onto the map. "It's a Hummer H2. Yellow."

"Of course it is," Ian muttered. "Which way did it go out of the truck stop?"

"East on I-40."

Ian grabbed one of the pens on the island. "Assuming he'll go the speed limit to avoid attracting attention, there's only so far he could have gone. Roadblocks can be set up within ten minutes. Accounting for speed and distance…" He mentally made the calculations, then drew a large circle that encompassed the truck stop and a large radius around it. "We'll need roadblocks here, here, here and here. And a lot of resources out searching." He glanced up. "Assuming you approve, of course. Boss?"

Nash rolled his eyes and grabbed his phone. "I'll take care of it."

Ian tossed the pen on the island and motioned his brothers to follow him into the great room. "The state troopers will be looking for him on the interstate. That's covered. Which means he'll exit soon, if not already, and end up on one of the roads I marked on the map. That's a lot of miles in between, from the truck stop to where they'll set up the barriers. And there's a lot of forest and rough terrain surrounding that area. With that Hummer, he could go off-road. I want to get out there and be a part of the search, try to figure out where he may have left the pavement. We'll need every man or woman we can get."

"Four main roads," Adam said. "Looks like we're splitting up again."

They agreed which roads they'd cover. Ian looked at each of his brothers in turn, then cleared his throat. "She means the world to me. I appreciate this, more than you know."

"Then we'd better find her," Adam said.

They took off running for the door.

Chapter Twenty-Five

Ian passed half a dozen Gatlinburg police cars on his way down the road that he'd chosen to search. He was relieved that so many of them were out looking for Shannon. But like him, they must not have found any evidence of the Hummer having come this way, or he'd have received a call.

He'd stopped at probably fifteen houses along the way doing knock and talks, seeing whether anyone had noticed the flashy yellow vehicle. But no one had. As he slowed to turn around at the roadblock to search this side road yet again, his phone buzzed in his pocket. He pulled to the shoulder and checked the screen. But he didn't recognize the number. "Special Agent McKenzie."

"This is Special Agent Bledzinski. Nash gave me your number."

"Did someone find her?"

"Uh, no, sir. Not that I know of. I'm still

here at the truck stop, interviewing potential witnesses while the techs comb the inside of the truck and—"

"Is this going somewhere, Bledzinski? I'm trying to find a missing woman."

"Sorry, sir. Yes, it's just, well, I got a call from one of the women we rescued, the one with the infant. You remember, she was the one who saw Miss Murphy. Well, an agent at the hospital patched her in on a conference line with me so we could talk and—"

"Bledzinski. Spit it out."

"Right. She said the suspect known as Wolverine said something odd to Miss Murphy. It was something along the lines of 'Smile. You're going to be on camera.' Does that mean anything to you?"

"You bet it does." He ended the call, flashed his badge and drove around the roadblock. At the next turnoff, he punched the number for Adam and sped down the two-lane road.

Adam answered on the first ring. "Ian, have you found her?"

"No, but I think I know where she is. Remember I told you about that warehouse outside of town, the one where I was supposed to do the exchange to free the women? There were cameras all over the place. And the yellow index card read, 'Smile for the camera.'

The woman who saw Shannon taken at the truck stop said the man who took her said, 'Smile. You're going to be on camera.' I think he's taken her there so he can—" he cleared his tight throat "—so he can film whatever he's going to do to her. He probably plans on sending it to me later, to make me suffer, after he makes his escape."

Adam swore. "Is Nash on the way with some agents?"

Ian made a sharp left onto another side road and slammed the accelerator again. The Charger's powerful engine whined as the car started up the mountain. "I haven't told Nash or the others yet. This may be my only chance to save her. I'm worried some yahoo will go in hot with lights and sirens, speed up the access road and be seen by Wolverine's cameras. This has to be done right, or she doesn't stand a chance. I want the element of surprise on my side. But I can't do this alone. I need someone I can trust."

"You can trust me, Ian. You can trust Colin and Duncan too. You know that, right?"

He turned another curve, then began to slow. "I do. I'm trusting all of you with Shannon's life. And mine. I need you to be my backup."

"Give me the address. I'll contact the others."

He gave him the address. He pulled his Charger to the side of the road and popped open the glove box. Being deep undercover rubbing elbows with bad guys had its perks, like owning a picklock set and knowing how to use it. He shoved the kit into his pocket and headed into the woods.

"I'm ten minutes from there," Adam said. "I just texted Duncan and Colin. They're even closer. We'll all rendezvous on the access road. I assume there's some tree cover close by so we can hoof it from there without being seen."

"There is. The best approach is behind the structure, the southwest corner." He hopped over a small ditch and jogged up the other side, then took off running again. "I don't remember any cameras back there since the lot doesn't run behind the building. That's where I'll come in, and where you guys can come in once you get there."

He crouched and carefully parted some bushes. Sure enough, a yellow Hummer sat boldly in the parking lot, right in front of the warehouse. He crept backward, then took off through the trees again, giving the parking lot and its cameras a wide berth.

"Ian, give me a call when you get there so we can coordinate our entry."

"I'm already here. Wolverine's Hummer is here too. I can't wait for backup." He ended the call and turned off the phone in case his brother called back. He didn't want the sound to give away his position. Then he leaped over the last ditch and ran to the back door of the building, picklock set in hand.

SHANNON STIFFENED AS Wolverine traced the knife across her throat, then used it to flick the ends of her hair.

"Blue tips." He snickered. "I suppose you consider yourself a rebel. A badass."

She strained against the zip ties that bound her to the folding chair in the middle of the room. "Cut me loose and find out. Just you and me. One-on-one."

He grinned and continued to circle the chair, running his knife across her hair, her shoulders, her legs, before stopping in front of her. "One-on-one time is what we're having right now. Aren't you enjoying it?" He leaned in closer. "I know your boyfriend will." He laughed and pointed toward the camera on the ceiling above her. "I want him to agonize over every…little…slice." He flicked the knife across her bare knees to emphasize each word, drawing more blood as he added to the dozens of cuts he'd already made.

Shannon sucked in a breath at the burning pain, biting her lip to keep from screaming. She knew that was what he wanted. And she wasn't about to give in. He wanted to send the video to Ian, her final moments. She prayed he'd never see it. But just in case he did, she wanted to make sure it was quick. She'd been baiting Wolverine since he'd enclosed her in this room and sent his men off to guard the warehouse. But no matter what she said, she couldn't seem to rattle him and make him just kill her and end his sick game.

His phone buzzed in his pocket. He frowned and pulled it out, studied the screen. Then he made a call. "Jack, Hulk, one of the sensors picked up something in the woods. Form a welcoming committee outside in the tree line. Blade, back hallway, southwest corridor. Keep an eye out. I think McKenzie might already be in the building. Remember, hurt him. But don't kill him."

Shannon made a choking sound in her throat.

He smiled, enjoying her fear. "Looks like I underestimated your boyfriend." He shoved the phone in his pocket. "He doesn't stand a chance against Blade." He grinned. "I really do love that name."

"Leave Ian alone," she gritted out between clenched teeth.

"Now, now. Don't look so worried. Blade knows that I want your lover to see the video before he dies. He'll just soften him up, get him ready. But he won't kill him. I get to do that. After he sees the video." He cocked his head. "Or should we do a live show for him? Draw him out in the open to make Blade's job easier? Then he can watch in real time as I carve you up." He drew back the knife and plunged it into her thigh.

A BLOOD-CURDLING SCREAM echoed in the warehouse. *Shannon.* The picklock kit fell from Ian's hands to the floor. The metal wands pinged across the concrete. He took off running through the maze of dark hallways toward the main part of the warehouse.

A light shone through a rectangular window in a door at the end of a hall. Ian ran to it. He could see the open part of the warehouse on the other side, all lit up, empty. And the only other rooms where Shannon could be were on the opposite side. Grasping his pistol in his left hand, he threw back the door and charged through the opening.

A flash of movement to his left had him whirling around. Something hard and solid came crashing down on his arm, sending his pistol clattering across the concrete floor and knocking Ian to the ground. He rolled over to face the threat. Blade. He glared down at Ian, a two-foot length of iron pipe in his right hand. He tapped it against his open palm and slowly approached.

Ian jerked his head back, searching for the pistol. Six feet away.

Blade roared and brought the pipe down in a lethal arc toward Ian's head.

Ian slammed his shoe against the other man's knee and dove to the side. Blade screamed with pain and rage as he crashed to the floor, but he still managed to swing the pipe toward Ian. He jerked out of the way, the whistle of the pipe just inches from his ear. It banged against the floor, showering both men in stinging flecks of chipped concrete.

Blade staggered to his feet and raised the pipe again.

On the other side of the warehouse, a pale face peered out through another glass cutout in one of the doors. Wolverine.

Blade roared.

Ian dove for his gun. The pipe slammed against his side. White-hot pain incinerated the breath in his lungs. Black spots swam before his eyes. His fingers cramped around the gun but he held on, fighting through the blinding pain to flop onto his back. He blinked furiously, trying to focus. Blade towered over him, lifting the pipe above his head. Ian twisted the pistol up toward him and squeezed the trigger. *Bam! Bam! Bam!*

The pipe dropped from Blade's hand. He stared in disbelief at Ian. Then his eyes rolled back in his head and he crumpled to the floor.

Ian struggled to draw air into his lungs as he fought through the haze of pain in his ribs. He looked across the warehouse toward the door. Wolverine jerked back from the glass.

A gunshot echoed outside. Two more followed in quick succession.

Another scream filled the warehouse.

Ian staggered to his feet and then took off in a pained crouch toward the door where he'd seen Wolverine.

"CHANGE OF PLANS," Wolverine snarled to Shannon. "Your boyfriend is here. You die *now*." He raised the knife above his head.

Ian was here? Shannon no longer wanted to die. She wanted, needed, to live, to keep this creep occupied to give Ian a better chance at survival.

The knife came down in a deadly arc.

She threw all her weight to the side, turning the chair over and crashing to the floor, the metal frame banging against the concrete.

Wolverine fell to the floor beside her, swearing as the knife clattered across the room and bounced against the far wall. Blood smeared his wrist where the knife had cut him as he fell. He glared at her, his face contorted with rage. "You'll pay for that."

A loud thump sounded against the door. "Shannon!" The doorknob rattled, but it was locked from the inside.

Shannon twisted around to see Ian banging his fist on the glass. "Ian!" She furiously strained against the plastic straps tying her to the chair. She had to let him inside or she'd die in here. She didn't want his last glimpse of her to be Wolverine stabbing her to death.

Wolverine swore and shoved to his feet. He ran across the room where the knife lay on the floor. Shannon rocked her body, scooting the chair toward the door as she struggled to pull her arms free.

"Cover your eyes!" Ian yelled.

She turned her head away from the door and squeezed her eyes shut.

Something slammed against the glass. It shattered, raining down onto the floor like pennies hitting a metal roof.

Wolverine twisted around on his knees, knife in hand.

Shannon looked back over her shoulder.

A shadow loomed behind Ian.

"Look out!" Shannon warned.

He jerked away from the small opening in the top of the door where the glass window had been. She couldn't see him. The sounds of grunting and bodies slamming against the door told of the violent struggle on the other side. She desperately shimmied and scooted, moving closer to the door.

Another shot echoed outside. Seconds later loud banging sounded from somewhere in the warehouse. Someone else was here. *Please let it be the police.* Her silent plea startled her, and she would have laughed if she weren't so terrified. Who would have thought she'd ever hope for the police to come help her?

Wolverine shouted his frustration and scrambled to his feet, holding the knife out in front of him.

Another loud thump sounded from outside. The door rattled in its frame.

Wolverine let out a terrifying war cry and ran toward Shannon.

The door burst open and slammed against the wall, an iron bar bouncing across the floor. Ian stumbled inside, a pistol clutched in his hand. He swung it toward Wolverine.

Bam!

Wolverine's body jerked, then fell to the

floor, his knife skittering over to land right in front of Shannon. His body went limp and his eyes closed. Blood began to seep out from underneath him.

"Shannon, oh my God. Shannon. How badly are you hurt?" Ian dropped to his knees beside her, setting down his pistol so he could run his hands frantically across the cuts on her arms and legs, smearing the blood as he tried to see how bad her injuries were.

"I'm okay." She grimaced when his hand touched the deep stab wound on her thigh.

Ian swore and took off his leather coat, wincing and moving awkwardly.

"You're hurt," she said. "Did you get shot?"

"I got hit by a truck."

"Oh, no, Ian!"

"Kidding. It just felt that way." He gently wrapped the coat around her thigh and tried to tie the sleeves together.

She gasped at the white-hot pain that shot through her leg.

He shot her a sympathetic look. "Sorry. Trying to stop the bleeding, but this stupid leather is too bulky." He looked around, then unbuckled his belt and wrapped it around her thigh, looping the ends together before stopping. "This is going to hurt. Bad. But it has to be done."

"I know. It's okay. Do it." She turned her face away, bracing herself. He jerked the belt tight. Blazing hot pain radiated up her body. She gulped in deep breaths, trying not to cry. But she couldn't help the whimper that escaped.

"All done," he told her, his voice hoarse. "Let me get those zip ties." He grabbed the knife and moved behind her.

The sounds of footsteps had both of them looking through the open doorway. Ian's brothers were running through the warehouse toward them.

Ian snorted. "The cavalry's here. A little late, but they still get points. I think they ran into Jack outside. He must have been tougher than he looked." He cut through the ties on Shannon's legs and moved to her hands.

She smiled up at him. A whisper of noise from the other side of the room had her jerking her head to the side.

Wolverine was staring at her, a mad light in his eyes as he brought up a pistol she hadn't even realized he had.

Ian dove over Shannon's body, throwing the knife like a javelin toward Wolverine.

Bam! Bam!

Wolverine dropped the gun and clawed at the hilt protruding from his neck.

Ian's brothers raced into the room, pistols out as they scanned for danger.

"Ian?" Shannon nudged him with her good leg. "Ian?" He lay on top of her, unmoving. "Ian!"

Adam ran to Wolverine's body and kicked his gun out of reach, then dropped to his knees to check his pulse.

Colin and Duncan raced to Ian and rolled him over.

Shannon gasped in horror at the bullet hole in his shirt. "Ian, damn you! When you said you'd jump in front of a bullet for me, I never actually wanted you to do it."

He groaned. His eyes fluttered open.

Hot tears ran down Shannon's face. "Oh my gosh, oh my gosh. Ian?"

"Ouuucch." He grimaced. "I don't know what hurts worse. Where Wolverine shot me or where Blade slammed an iron pipe against my ribs."

The two brothers exchanged a glance. Then Colin pulled out a pocketknife and moved behind Shannon.

"Ian's been shot?" Adam rushed over to them, his phone to his ear. "I've got an ambulance and police on the way. Wolverine won't be hurting anyone else. He's gone." He got down on his knees beside his brother.

Shannon willed Ian to look at her, but he stared straight up at the ceiling. "Ian, talk to me. Say something."

"What's that crackling sound every time I breathe?"

"I think it's your ribs." Duncan grasped Ian's shirt and ripped it open. "God bless whoever invented bullet-resistant vests."

The plastic ties around Shannon's wrists fell away, and Colin moved to check on Ian. Shannon reached for him, but Duncan stopped her and gently pushed her down on her back. "Sorry, lass. You're bleeding from a couple dozen different places. We need to get the bleeding under control."

"How bad are her wounds?" Ian's voice sounded oddly weak.

"Bad enough. How far out is that ambulance, Adam?"

Shannon blinked up at Duncan. He was pressing against her wounds, but she couldn't feel anything. Except...cold, so very, very cold.

"ETA ten minutes." Adam leaned over Shannon, his brow furrowed with concern. "Don't worry. The ambulance will be here soon."

"Guys," Colin called out, sounding worried. "I don't think all the blood on the floor is from Shannon."

Adam leaned over Ian, running his hands up and down his shirt. He froze, then met Colin's gaze. "One of the bullets missed the vest. It went in through the arm opening."

"Ian?" Shannon called out, except it sounded fuzzy to her ears. "Ian?"

Adam swore. "We're losing both of them. Duncan, keep pressure on her wounds. Colin, call 911 again. Tell them we need a medevac chopper out here."

While Adam stripped off his coat and then balled up his shirt to stanch the bleeding, Shannon stretched her fingers toward Ian. She entwined them with his and squeezed.

He didn't squeeze back.

Chapter Twenty-Six

Shannon leaned back on her crutches beside one of the massive outdoor heaters, doing her best to blend into the background of the massive tent. The McKenzies were across the way in a receiving line, shaking hands with the last of their wedding guests as they said their goodbyes. Ian glanced at her, looking more handsome than ever in his black tuxedo, even sitting in a wheelchair.

She'd teased him about dyeing his hair back to its natural black color, telling him he might have to turn over his rebel card. He'd insisted that he'd only done it so that he'd match the tuxedo better. Just like she'd chosen to wear a blue dress to match the blue tips of her hair. If she didn't know better, she'd think he was developing a sense of humor, much like his brother Duncan.

Since the shooting a little over two weeks ago, Ian had definitely been smiling more than she was used to seeing. He seemed happier, less tense. And she didn't think that it was because the case he'd been working on was wrapped up. It was all about being reunited with his family, especially his father. They had a long way to go to heal years of hurts between them. But they were well on their way.

He winked and turned back to shake the hand of some senator or representative, or maybe it was a judge. She'd lost track of all the dignitaries who had attended the double-wedding ceremony of Colin to Peyton and Duncan to Remi. The Christmas weddings had been amazing, taking place in the building a few feet away from the tent. The family called it a barn, even though it had never been used to house any animals.

The barn's interior was rustic, but homey, filled to bursting with strands of white party lights and red poinsettias to go along with the holiday-themed occasion. Everything had been perfect, especially Ian's family. They'd been so kind and welcoming, as if she was one of them.

She and Ian had both been staying at his parents' cabin, although in separate bedrooms, while they recovered from their injuries. A home-care nurse stopped by daily to check on both of them, but mainly she was there for Ian. Wolverine's bullet had tumbled around inside his chest and done enormous damage. And Blade had shattered two of Ian's ribs. It would take a long time for him to heal.

Shannon's injuries had been far less severe. The blood loss had nearly killed her, and she'd needed surgery to repair the lacerated muscles in her thigh. But all of her other cuts had been paltry compared to what Ian had suffered. Tomorrow morning, she was returning to the duplex.

Ian had insisted she could stay with him at his parents' home as long as she wanted. She'd given him some lame excuse about being homesick. In reality her savings were pretty much wiped out, and she desperately needed to get another job. She couldn't afford to stay here any longer, even though she would have loved to continue to be by Ian's side. Thankfully, a victim's fund had covered her medical bills or she would have had those hanging over her head too.

Now that the guests were gone, the McKenzies surprised Shannon by returning to the barn instead of going up to the family's cabin.

Ian maneuvered his motorized wheelchair until he was directly in front of Shannon.

"Hey, pretty lady," he teased. "Did you have fun tonight?"

"You know I did, handsome man. I only hyperventilated twice, when the police chief shook my hand and when your boss stopped to chat with me."

"You'll get over your law enforcement phobia yet."

She smiled. "Some of them aren't that bad." She leaned down and pressed a soft kiss against his cheek.

He grinned. "Whatever I did to deserve that, tell me so I can do it again."

"Your boss said you'd donated the use of your cabin as a temporary halfway house for the human trafficking victims. You're an amazing man, Ian McKenzie."

He shrugged, looking uncomfortable with her praise. "Yeah, well. It sits there empty most of the time. Might as well serve some kind of purpose. Besides, once I met your Maria, and found out she was actually Willow Rivera, I had to do something to help her get a new start in life. I'd already failed her all those years ago. I'm just glad her stepfather lied and she was still alive. Had I known, I would have—"

"You would have joined Homeland Security and dedicated your life to helping others? I think you can let go of all that guilt, Ian. You did everything that can be done and more. You've done far more to help other people than most ever dream of doing. Maria—Willow—is happy and healthy. And now she can look forward to giving her baby girl the life she never had for herself. You did that, Ian. You and you alone."

He stared at her intently, but didn't say anything.

Beginning to feel uncomfortable, she forced a laugh and waved toward the barn. "I assumed your family would head up to the house. Why did they go back inside the barn?"

"Pictures. Mom wanted to snap some of her own on her phone so she can post them on social media without having to wait for the professional photos. You'll join us, won't you?"

"Of course. I'd love to." She reached for his hand, but instead of turning the wheelchair and heading up the path, he jerked her forward and caught her in his lap, knocking her crutches to the ground. "Ian, what are you doing? I could hurt your ribs and—"

"My ribs are wrapped so tight I can barely

breathe. Trust me. There's no way you could hurt them."

He pushed the button on his wheelchair and carried her forward until they were in front of the barn's massive entrance, which was standing wide open. His family was smiling and laughing inside at the other end as his mother snapped pictures.

Shannon smiled and looked up at Ian. "I love your family. I'm going to miss them terribly."

He gently cupped her face. "They love you too. So do I."

She blinked against the rush of tears that burned the backs of her eyes. "Don't."

He frowned. "Don't tell you I love you?"

She twisted her hands in her lap. "It's cruel. As soon as you're healed, you'll go back to work and disappear deep undercover on another case. I'll probably never see you again."

He gently tilted her chin up so she would look at him. "Explain to me how it's cruel that I tell you I'm in love with you."

A single tear slipped down her cheek. "You know why," she whispered.

He smiled tenderly. "I think so. But I need you to tell me, to be sure."

She shoved his hand away and stared down at her lap again. "Because I'm in love with you too." She drew a ragged breath. "There. I said it. Okay? We love each other and it doesn't matter."

"Then I wasted a lot of money on this for nothing."

She jerked her head up, then froze. He was holding a gorgeous pear-shaped diamond solitaire ring on a band of white gold. And the diamond wasn't like any other diamond she'd ever seen. She drew a sharp breath and pressed her hand against her throat. "It's…blue."

He laughed, his eyes sparkling. "To match your hair." He gently brushed the tears from her cheeks. "I thought I knew what I wanted, and then I met you and realized I'd been fooling myself all these years. I've been running away from the very things that matter most— family, belonging and, most important, love. I love you, Shannon. You gave me back my family. You gave me acceptance, hope and love before I even knew that's what I needed. *You're* what I need. And it took almost losing you for me to understand that. Marry me, Shannon. Marry me and make me the happiest man in the world. And I swear that I'll do everything I can to make you happy too."

She drew another ragged breath and shook her head. "I can't."

His smile faded, and he slowly lowered his hands to his lap. "Why? We love each other."

"Because I don't want you to hate me years down the road when you look back and realize you gave up the career that you'd worked so hard for, because of me. You're an amazing special agent. You love the work you do. I couldn't bear it if I took that away from you."

He cupped her face again, the ring sparkling where he'd shoved it on the end of his thumb. "What I want is you, and everything that comes with that. A home, whatever kind of house or cabin you want. And babies. I want babies with your gorgeous green eyes and jet-black hair. The blue tips can wait until their teenage years."

She drew a ragged breath again. "You're being cruel again."

"No, I'm putting all my cards on the table. I'm going all in to get what I want. Because we both want the same things. We want a life we can be proud of, a life we can build with each other. And I want to get to know my family again. That means being here, not running off for months and years. I don't have to be a special agent working undercover to help others. All I have to do is open my checkbook. Think about it, Shannon. If you can't marry me for love, marry me for money. You can help me use it to build real halfway houses and help victims of human trafficking and other horrors far more than I could as a special agent."

She stared at him in shock, too afraid to hope. "You really want to do all that?"

He nodded. "I do."

"Then the answer is no. I can't marry you for your money." This time she cupped his face in her hands. "But I will marry you for love." She leaned forward and kissed him.

He growled deep in his throat and deepened the kiss, threading his fingers through her hair and showing her just how much he loved her and wanted her.

"Um, excuse me. Does this mean she said yes?" Adam called out.

Shannon broke the kiss, her face flushing with heat when she saw that all of Ian's family was watching them from inside.

Ian held up the ring. "Well?"

She grinned and held up her hand. He slid the ring on her finger and kissed her again.

His family cheered and clapped.

"Hurry up," his father called out. "The governor only swore me in as a temporary judge until midnight. If I'm officiating, we have to do this in the next few minutes."

Ian drew back, laughing.

Shannon stared at his family, who'd all suddenly lined up at the front as if they were a wedding party. And his father was standing behind the podium with a Bible on top, just like he'd done hours earlier when he'd officiated at his other sons' weddings.

"A surprise wedding, Ian? You planned this?"

"Let's just say I was really, really hoping. I didn't want you to leave tomorrow and go back to the duplex. What do you say?" He searched her gaze. "I was banking on your love of the unconventional. But if you prefer to wait and get a white wedding dress and—"

She pressed her fingers against his mouth. "No. This is perfect, better than anything I could ever hope for. I love you, Ian. More than you could possibly imagine. I love you, and I want to marry you right this minute."

"That's good," his father called out. "Because that's about all we have left. Hurry!"

Ian pressed the button on his wheelchair and zipped up the aisle. Shannon laughed as she held on to the arms of the chair to keep from falling against his chest and hurting him.

"I do," he said, as soon as they were in front of his father.

Laughing, Shannon said, "I do too."

His father blinked and looked around, then shrugged. "Then I guess I pronounce you husband and wife. Go on. Kiss or whatever." He rolled his eyes and closed the Bible.

Ian's family cheered and surrounded them as he planted a laughing, sloppy kiss against her lips.

* * * * *

*Look for more books from
Lena Diaz coming soon!*

*And don't miss the previous books in
The Mighty McKenzies miniseries:*

Smoky Mountains Ranger
Smokies Special Agent
Conflicting Evidence

Available now from Harlequin Intrigue!